DEATH'S STORM

THE DIVINITIES
BOOK TWO

LIA DAVIS

Death's Storm

The Divinities, book 2

© copyright 2016 Lia Davis

Published by Davis Raynes Publishing Group, LLC

PO Box 224 | Middleburg, Fl. 32050

Cover by and Formatting by Glowing Moon Designs

www.AuthorLiaDavis.com

DEATH'S STORM

A desire he's never felt before could be more dangerous than the demons out to destroy them.

Technical genius and demi-goddess—a.k.a Divinity—Khloe Bradenton relies on no one for help, and she definitely doesn't need comfort from anyone but her twin. After her parents were killed by the demons over two years ago, she graciously accepts her role in the war between the demons and witches. But when a creature far more dangerous than the ones responsible for killing her parents claims he is her guardian and steps in with help she never asked for, she is torn between her desire for the dark predator and memories of the painful loss she endured at the hands of her enemies and from those who claimed to love her in the past.

One of the last Death Demons still in existence,

Jagger has pledged his life to the Goddess of Witchcraft, Hecate. Charged with guardianship of the Divinities—one particular spitfire, in particular—he was told never to approach them, but simply to aid from a distance. But when Khloe sacrifices herself to save her twin and best friend and thus becomes the demons' prey, Jagger has no choice but to reveal himself to her. However, he is taken by surprise when the desire to claim her as his own emerges, and his need for her burns hotter than her Fire. But in the midst of the war, their feelings for each other could prove more dangerous than the demons out to destroy them.

CHAPTER ONE

Chaos was working overtime.

Buildings burned, many with flames about ten stories high. People ran, screaming, in all directions. Children cried in the distance. The thick, inky feel of black magic hung in the air like a wet blanket.

Khloe's heart ached at the scene. She stood in the center of the Maxville Coven. Only it wasn't present day—that she was sure.

"Connie?" Noah, a Divinity Elder and close friend of Khloe's parents, spoke softly, his voice carrying to her despite the noise around her. "Can you help Vanessa with the little ones?"

Khloe jerked around at the sound of her mother's name. "Mom," she breathed as she spotted her mother as a teenager. Connie nodded at Noah and immediately directed the children to go with her. Beside her was

Vanessa Manus—Noah's wife and the current priestess of the Maxville Coven.

Tears burned Khloe's eyes. They were so young.

An explosion, like a large ass bomb, sounded several blocks ahead of where she stood. Khloe jumped, noting her mother and Vanessa rushing into a house with the children. Somehow, she'd been transported back in time. To when the Maxville Coven had been attacked by Khan and his demons—when the Divinities had gained their powers.

Noah had told them the story, but to see it in the flesh was surreal.

A surge of power cut through the air, making the hairs on her arms stand on end. Turning, Khloe watched as Hecate appeared in front of Noah, Kristoff, and Melaina. "Are you ready, my children?"

The shock on their faces told Khloe they hadn't expected her. They went down on their knees and bowed their heads without question. "Yes, Goddess."

"Then stand and let's kick some ass," she prompted.

A group of demons flashed in at that moment, then stalked toward them like a wave. Noah narrowed his eyes and thrust his hands straight out in front of him toward the demons. White light left his palms and hit the first couple of demons, sending them flying backwards into the fiends behind them.

Stunned, he studied his hands as if he didn't know he possessed that power. He lifted his gaze to Hecate. Khloe followed his stare and saw the goddess engaging four demons. They charged her two at a time, and then all four at once. She was too fast for them, Khloe mused before Hecate took a hit in the side that made her cry out. Khloe's heart skipped a beat. When Noah made a move to go to her, the goddess spoke, stopping him. "Don't worry about me. Use your magic. Think about what you want and will it so."

He glanced at Kris and Mel, who nodded as if they too had heard Hecate's command. As a unit, they rushed the demons with powers no normal witch possessed. Although the god-like magic was new to the three Divinity Elders, Khloe had known it her whole life. Well, as long as she could remember. The ability to connect to the elements had always been with Khloe. The power increasing as she grew up.

A roar cut through the night, stealing Khloe's attention and shifting it to Kristoff as one of the demons swiped a sword across his back. A fierce growl ripped from him as he whirled around to face the demon. His eyes glowed amber like dancing flames. Khloe had heard stories of shifters and knew from her mother that Kristoff was a white tiger. However, she'd never seen him shift. By the way his eyes glowed, and his skin tightened, she guessed she was about to.

"Back off!" Kris called out. Noah and Mel backed off slightly. When they did, Kris threw his hands out in front of him and then spread them wide, sending flames out like a blowtorch to encircle the group of demons.

Khloe smiled while her own hands itched. Fire was her favorite element. Plus, she hated being there, seeing them fight, and not being able to join them.

A moment later, Noah stepped up and raised his arms. The vines covering the trees snaked along the ground, unseen by the demons until they took hold, twining and twisting and wrapping around the demons' legs up to their torsos.

Mel took that opportunity to call her element. A light breeze picked up, blowing Kris's Fire toward the demons and feeding the flames.

All together, they sent everything they had into what they'd created. The vines twined around while the air intensified the flames and pushed them over the demons, burning them all in a matter of minutes.

Everything fell quiet. Khloe watched with amazement as Hecate walked toward the three. She was still as beautiful as she had been before the fight began. Then again, she was a goddess. She stopped in front of them and held out an amulet of some kind. About five inches in diameter, it was too big to be worn as a piece of jewelry, but Khloe knew what it was. She also noted that it looked slightly bigger than the one they'd recovered last month.

The center of the amulet was a crystal sphere that seemed to glow with multi-colored energy waves. Surrounding the sphere was a labyrinth-like symbol: Hecate's Wheel, the symbol of knowledge and life.

"This is the Sinew. It is the source of all magic and

knowledge. Guard it with your lives. The demons must never have it again." Hecate gave them the Sinew and vanished.

Suddenly, everything faded, like Khloe's surroundings just dissolved away. A moment later, she stood in a living room that she didn't recognize.

A woman's painful cries echoed from the hallway. Khloe rushed to a bedroom at the end of the hall and froze at the doorway. Paul Loomis—a demon living as a human and the father of Kalissa's ex-boyfriend—knelt on his knees, holding his very pregnant wife, Barbra's, hand as she gave birth to their child.

The midwife delivered the child, wrapped it in a towel, and started to leave the room when Barbra called out to her. "I want to see him. Why can't I see my son?"

Panic set in, creasing her forehead and making her shake. Paul tried to calm his wife, then said, "Bring the boy here."

Khloe had always hated the man, even before she'd found out that he was a demon. Moving closer to Barbra, Khloe snuck a peek at the child she knew all too well was Liam Loomis—the male who'd stolen her twin's memories to keep her from her true magical partner and the love of her life. The demon had taken precious time from Kalissa and Ayden all because Liam wanted Khloe's sister for himself. Sick bastard.

"Why does he look like that? Is he okay?" Barbra's panicked tone made Khloe glance at the baby again.

Her heart skipped a few beats. It wasn't the slight blueish coloring of his skin, but the black rose on the inside of his left forearm that caught Khloe's attention.

A Dark Divine. Half witch, half demon.

Just then, Paul's head snapped up and turned in her direction as if he could see her. Impossible. Wasn't it? After all, it was *her* dream. He narrowed his gaze and snarled with a curled lip.

Fear froze in her gut as her father's face flashed in her mind. Tears stung her eyes, and her nose tingled. *Dad.* When she reached out to him, he transformed into a black leopard and leapt at her, teeth bared.

She screamed. Her magic ran wild within, and the flares from her connection to the Fire element sparked to life. A moment later, wind blasted through the windows and glass shattered around them. "You killed them!"

"Khloe. Damn it. Ayden."

"Kalissa?" Khloe heard her sister, but she couldn't see her. She sounded so far away.

"I'm here. But you have to calm down. Let go of the vision." Kalissa didn't make any sense? What vision? She didn't have that gift.

A moment later, Ayden materialized in front of her and gripped her shoulders, flames crawled up his arms, but it didn't harm him. He was using his Divinity gift of adaptability—the ability to use others' powers.

"Lo, listen to me. This isn't real."

She blinked then glanced over his shoulder to Paul,

who bent to kiss Barbra on the forehead. Meeting Ayden's stare, she frowned. "They killed them."

"Not them." He pointed to Paul and Barbra. "Khan ordered it done, and we'll catch him."

Yes, they would. "I don't know how to get out of this."

Ayden smiled, and her surroundings shifted again. When the room came into view, relief flooded her as she recognized her own bedroom. She glanced to Kalissa. "Are your visions always like that?"

"No." She paused, drawing her brows together. "I'll put coffee on, and we can try to make sense of it."

Khloe stared at the ceiling and slowed her racing heart. A tightening in her chest matched Kalissa's concern that brushed against Khloe's subconscious. And Ayden didn't help by closing off his emotions. Sometimes it sucked being linked to an empath.

Khloe glared at the red digital numbers on the stove clock. 5:00 AM. She was never up before nine. "How did I get sucked into a dream vision?"

Kalissa handed her a cup of coffee, then sat across

from her at the small kitchen table. "I'm not sure. Maybe because it isn't your gift."

"I don't know what it means. Why me?" Khloe sipped her coffee and sighed as the dark, robust but sweet taste hit her tongue. None of it made any sense. Why would her dad change into a leopard?

"I'm not sure." Kalissa repeated, then offered, "The Fates could have chosen you for a journey."

The Fates can suck it. Khloe was just fine on the path she was on. Hunting demons and finding out how to go to the Underworld to kill Khan.

Ayden leaned against the counter and nodded. "Could be one that brings the past to the future or something."

"Oh, well, that sure clears things up." Khloe rolled her eyes and sagged in her chair. It was great that she didn't have to explain the visions to either of them. They were bound, times two. Because Khloe shared a psychic connection with her twin, when Kalissa and Ayden mated—binding their magic and lives together—Khloe had been dragged in with them. It wasn't in a creepy threesome way. It was more like Ayden had joined the twin connection.

Then they were bound to Hecate and the other two Divinities, Lydia and Melaina, as well as Zach—Ayden's cousin and one of Khloe's best friends. Zach was also the grandson of one of the Divinity Elders, Noah Manus.

"I don't like the vague hints of what they think my

future holds." Khloe hated structure, most of the time anyway. She didn't want to know what the future held. And she definitely didn't want the Fates playing with the path she was supposed to travel.

"I don't think it's something we need to worry about right now. For all we know, it could be a sign of what Khan is cooking up." Kalissa stood and yawned. "I'm going back to bed. We promised to take Lydia shopping today."

Khloe smiled. Even though she wasn't a huge fan of shopping, she did love spending time with her sister and her new best friend. "I may stay up. I'm too wired to sleep right now."

As Divinities, they didn't need much sleep. The enhanced magic in their blood kept them young and energized. The only time Khloe ever remembered getting tired was when she used up large amounts of energy, which had been a month ago when Liam kidnapped Kalissa, and Khloe and the others went in to save her.

Damn demons. Lightning cracked over the house as Khloe's anger toward the Underworld servants spiked within her. Her emotions were too closely tied to her elemental gifts.

"Khloe."

She laughed at her sister's warning tone coming from the downstairs master suite Kalissa and Ayden stayed in. "I'm fine. Go to sleep."

Cupping her coffee in her hands, she glanced out

the window. They needed to find out what Khan had planned. Things had been too quiet in the last month. No demon attacks, no threats.

Khloe knew something was coming. And she was ready.

CHAPTER TWO

*T*here it was again. The creepy, dark feeling of being watched. The awareness was always there since Kalissa's kidnapping, but this was different. Darker. Khloe had first felt it about an hour ago. It followed them like a black storm cloud hovering overhead.

Khloe exited the last clothing store for the day, relieved to be heading home. At least she was glad to get her twin sister and her new BFF away from whatever or whoever was watching them. She tested a theory that she was the one being watched by wandering away from the other women. Not too far away, just enough to know if the feeling lessened. Khloe never let her sister and Lydia out of her sight.

The entity followed her. It even seemed to get closer to her the farther away from the others she got. *Interesting.*

The three of them were Divinities—witches born with extra, god-like abilities—and could take care themselves. Even Lydia being eight months pregnant could defend herself as much as the others. However, after Khloe and Kalissa's parents were killed almost two years ago, they'd found themselves thrown in the middle of an ancient war between witches and demons.

A war where the Divinities were the front line, protecting both the *magickin* and humans from the Underworld demon lord, Khan. The demon wanted the Sinew—a crystal sphere that held the magic of the three worlds.

Khloe was happy to hunt the bastard down and stop him.

Shaking off the thoughts of war, Khloe glanced at Lydia and frowned. The other Divinity had tied her long, red hair up in a ponytail about halfway through the shopping trip, complaining about the heat. Khloe dismissed it as one of Lydia's prego hot flashes that she often had. After all, it was early March, and the air still held the crisp winter coolness. For Florida, it was like a second Fall.

However, the fatigue settling over Lydia's porcelain features was starting to worry Khloe. "Are you okay?"

Lydia shifted her green-and-blue gaze to Khloe and smiled. "I'm fine."

With a sigh, Khloe looked at Kalissa, shrugged, and let the subject drop. Lydia kept her emotions on a tight leash, not letting anyone see her pain. Being able to pick up each other's emotions was one of the benefits of having been bound together a month ago by the Goddess of Witchcraft, Hecate. It was a blessing, *and* very annoying. Especially when it was Khloe who tried to rein in her emotions. They were heavily tied to her Divinity gift to control the weather and the natural elements so she had to.

Beyond the wall Lydia hid behind was a lot of pain and even more rage. Khloe understood the anger and the need to hide the pain from others. Lydia hadn't only lost her father and husband, her mother was missing, and she was possibly in the hands of the demons. Hell, Lydia was handling it a lot better than Khloe would in her shoes. Then again, she wasn't the one about to be a mother, so she didn't know what it was like to possess the maternal instinct to love, protect, and be strong for the sake of a child. Still, it wasn't healthy to keep everything bottled up inside.

"We can relax in the hot tub when we get home," Khloe said, moving ahead of the other two women.

"That would be nice," Lydia replied with a real smile this time, not the forced I'm-not-hiding-my-pain smile she usually offered everyone.

Stepping off the curb to head to the car, Khloe stilled and let the cool air caress her skin. An electrical charge that only the select few *magickin*—like her and the other Divinities—could detect was palpable in the early spring air.

Her spine tingled as another supernatural energy drifted on the wind, putting her on full alert. Reaching out with her senses, she relaxed. A little. The power was familiar in an odd kind of way. Her admirer was nearby. Was he the one following them, hiding his signature?

More like a stalker, really, without the creepy love letters and phone calls.

For the last month, someone had watched her and followed her every move. When the entity was near, a warm shiver rolled over her skin like a caress. The energy didn't come from a human. Demon? Maybe. But the power was too intense to be any demonic creature she'd come in contact with. She considered one of the gods, but that didn't make sense either. The gods wouldn't stalk her. They would send a messenger or deliver their message in person. She and the others had also thought it could be a guardian.

Whatever the entity was, it annoyed the hell out of her to be followed around and spied upon.

She scanned the mall parking lot and the sidewalk that led to the various shops. Nothing remotely threatening came into view or reached out to her supernatural senses. Then again, she never saw anything when she felt the presence. It had shown up last month, right after Kalissa had been kidnapped by Kalissa's ex and discovered their destiny to fight in the war.

That was when she and her sister had found a note from their mother telling them about the Sinew, and had sent Kalissa on a mission to retrieve it. As Divinities, it was their duty to protect *magickin* from Khan, the new bastard Lord of the Underworld.

Khloe gladly pledged to take a stand in the war. After all, it was Khan and his demonic army who'd taken her parents away from her almost two years ago. She was going to make them pay, no matter how long it took. Being long-lived, time was something she had plenty of.

The wind picked up, bringing the scent of coming rain. She looked up, inhaled, and smiled. Dark storm clouds filled the afternoon sky. She loved storms. Being able to call upon the elements and bend them to her will was her Divine gift. So, she took every opportunity she could to enjoy them. "There's a powerful storm headed our way."

"It's a good thing we're going straight home." Kalissa reached out to snatch Khloe's cell from her.

She jerked away before Kalissa could grab it, laughed, and jogged ahead of the other two women. Kalissa's blond curls, a shade darker than Khloe's and without pink streaks, were pulled back in a ponytail, but it was the annoyance across her slightly oval face that made Khloe giggle with mischief. Walking backward in the direction of Kalissa's new Beamer, Khloe scrolled through the pictures she had snapped of them shopping. Her twin hated having her picture taken and would delete the photos once she got ahold of the phone. No way. Khloe had plans for these babies, like uploading them to the *magickin* social network, Magical Enchantments.

"Lo, stop."

Khloe froze and snapped her head up to meet Kalissa's violet, anxious gaze. The psychic connection to her twin told her she wasn't talking about the phone. Hairs stood up on the back of her neck, and a shiver rolled down her spine. A new demonic power touched her awareness—different, colder than their daily stalker.

"Here." She shoved her shopping bags at Kalissa and put the cell in the back pocket of her shorts. "You and Lydia head home. I'll catch up to you."

Kalissa shook her head. "I don't like this."

Neither did she, but they had gone over it. The plan was that anytime they were out and shit got critical, they'd split up. When her sister had bonded with and married the sheriff of Maxville, Ayden Daniels, the connection between Ayden and Kalissa extended through the twin bond to Khloe. All three of them could connect telepathically and emotionally now, and the three of them could use the gift to tap into other magical beings' powers. To keep the gift from falling into Khan's hands, they agreed they should never be caught together, because together, they were both more powerful and also more vulnerable.

Khan would drain them of their magic, which would kill them instantly because a Divinity's magic was tied to their life force. They couldn't survive without it. Khan would then use that magic in his plans to merge the natural world and the Afterworld to the Underworld.

Today, they'd taken a huge risk with Lydia. She was eight months pregnant and, according to the *magickin* birth cycle, was due any day.

"Look, you said yourself that our stalker might be a guardian sent to watch over us. If that's the case, then I'm not alone."

"That's just a hunch. We're not sure."

"Please, Lis. Go. I'll be okay."

Kalissa let out a heavy sigh and urged Lydia in front of her to shield the other Divinity from harm as they rushed toward the car.

The squealing of tires and the sight of a white minivan barreling toward them sent Khloe's heart into marathon speed. She gave her sister and her new best friend a kiss on their cheeks and took off through the parking lot, hoping the demon would take the bait.

She glanced over her shoulder to the BWM. Kalissa and Lydia were safe inside and pulling out of the parking space. Thank the gods. A pang of relief rolled through her, and she prayed Kalissa and Lydia would make it home safely.

"Adyen, Kalissa is on her way home. Make sure she gets there. Don't ask. I'll be fine!" Khloe sent the telepathic message to her brother-in-law then closed the mental connection, shielding her thoughts.

The roar of an engine drew her attention to the white box on wheels speeding toward her, much too fast for a parking lot. It was closing in. She hit the sidewalk and ran toward the road. She wanted to lead them out of the city limits without becoming the next demon delicacy. The farther away from witnesses, the better. They had enough to deal with because of the demons. They didn't need a twenty-first century lynch mob to contend with, too.

A quick glance at the advancing vehicle caused her heart to slam against her ribcage. The van's side door slid open, and a demon jumped out, tucked his head, and rolled across the pavement into the grass. He jumped up and ran straight for her.

Shit!

She pushed her legs as fast as they could go. The racing engine of the van grew louder. She flashed a couple of miles up the road. Without a set destination, she couldn't teleport far. Where would she go anyway?

Outrunning that damn van wasn't happening. She might be a powerful witch, but she didn't know where she could go or how many demons were packed inside that van. Judging by the strength and power rolling off the ones chasing her, they were *Amiddians,* the middle-class citizens of the Underworld.

She whirled and thrust an energy ball at the demon, knocking him backward a few feet. Quickly, she threw a softball size fireball at him. It hit him square in the chest. The flames covered his body and, within seconds, he disappeared into a pile of ash.

Squealing tires followed by the crunching and

scraping of metal on pavement behind her sparked her curiosity. Her nose tingled at the smell of hot brakes and burnt rubber. When she turned to look at the wreckage, she gasped. The van lay on its side in the middle of the street. A much stronger and larger male, with hair black as night and long enough to allow fingers to comb through it, stood at the front of the vehicle, his massive chest rose and fell under his black T-shirt as he took deep, calculated breaths.

After punching through the glass, he reached inside the windshield and pulled out the driver. A force of power rolled off the newcomer unlike anything Khloe had ever felt before. He didn't radiate demon magic like the others. Although his aura was dark, his power was almost godly. And familiar.

Her stalker.

His power reached out to her like the physical caress of a lover, sending tingles over her skin. His sculpted body moved in a sensual, yet deadly manner. Her hands itched to touch him, to feel his warm skin under her palms. She closed her eyes to stop the urge to go to him, shivered, and then cursed her body for responding to him. Usually, demons threw off eerie, frigid energy. But, this one, he warmed her in a way no man had ever done.

Okay, Lo. You have officially lost your mind.

The *Amiddian*, held off the ground in the death grip of her stalker, kicked his legs wildly and screamed as the larger male spoke in tones too low for her to make out the words. She caught a glimpse of huge, sharp fangs before he latched on to his victim's neck.

For the love of the gods...

After a few moments, Mr. Tall Dark and Scary tossed the lifeless body away like last week's trash and turned toward her. She swallowed hard.

His attention snapped to the left. Khloe followed his gaze to another demon running toward her. Her stalker flashed to stand in front of the other demon, and she fled in the opposite direction.

She was so not hanging around to see what he did to that one. Cutting to her right, she ran into the woods, away from her stalker and her would-be captors.

Several feet inside the undeveloped property, another demon materialized in front of her. She dug her heels into the ground to keep from plowing into him. White-blond hair framed his too-thin demonic face. Most demons looked human, allowing them the ability to blend into the natural world. This one didn't blend very well. At least not to her. For one, his crimson-colored eyes were anything but human. Secondly, his dark magic rolled off him in powerful, choking waves.

Heart hammering in her ears, she darted to the side, but he was too fast for her. His large, rough hands wrapped around her upper arm, and his sharp claws dug into her skin, making her cry out. As quickly as he'd grabbed her, an iron bracelet was snapped around her wrist. The cuff he'd put on her right arm instantly muted her magic. Fear sliced through her gut. The flow of energy within her slowed and backed away from the iron, not wanting to touch it. She tried to force it out, create a spark, but it didn't work. Even her elemental magic receded. *Damn.* She was powerless against him.

Panic gripped her, and she struggled against the large demon. Her survival instincts kicked in, and she brought her foot up and thrust it out, right into his groin. With a painful groan, he crumpled to the ground.

It was a good thing male demons had the same weaknesses as human men. Take out the jewels, and women could rule the world.

The warm tingle across her skin said her stalker was closing in on her, and she bolted deeper into the woods.

Jagger tossed the *Amiddian* to the side, stepped away from the overturned van, and froze. Khloe stood on the shoulder of the road about fifty feet ahead, watching him. Her pink-streaked blond hair framed her oval face, making her look like a pissed off angel. He took a step forward and felt the dark presence of another demon. He jerked his gaze to the new energy to see a horned, blue-skinned demon advancing on Khloe.

Fuck. Where were they coming from?

Letting out a low growl, Jagger materialized in front of the demon and grabbed him by the front of his shirt. The creature snarled and snapped his teeth. Jagger released his power over the demon, showing him what true hell his death could be. As a Death Demon, Jagger could make the male die as fast or slow as Jagger wished. Today was the demon's lucky day. Jagger didn't have time to play. So he would die quickly.

Holding the hell-spawn off the ground, Jagger let his fangs drop. "What do you want with her?"

The demon narrowed his eyes and smirked, but said nothing.

Tightening his grip, Jagger gave the demon one more chance. Using telepathy, Jagger reached into his mind and squeezed. "You can tell me, or I'll drain the memories from your useless soul."

The idiot laughed and vanished.

Fuck! No one should have been able to flash from his hold. He surrounded them with a spell for just that reason. There was only one possibility. Khan had a power source just like Jagger suspected.

Fisting his hands at his sides, he whirled around to

find Khloe gone. Great. Another complication. Scenting the air, he picked up on her chocolate-rose fragrance and rushed into the forest. He found her several feet into the trees and brush.

She wasn't alone. A *Regal*—the imperial guards of Khan and the most powerful demons in the Underworld—stood over her with his hand gripping her arm.

Rage ran hot in Jagger's veins, fueling his need to protect her and kill for her.

He soon discovered his Khloe was a fireball. She kicked the *Regal* in the balls, taking the demon to the ground. Turning on her heels, she took off again, but not before he caught the scent of blood.

A deep growl ripped from his throat, and he thrust his hand toward the male struggling to stand, hitting him with a ball of hellfire, compliments of Hecate. The demon puffed into a black pile of dust.

No one harmed what belonged to him and lived.

CHAPTER THREE

*K*hloe stopped running. She hunched over with her hands on her knees and listened. The only thing she heard was her own heavy breathing. With the coming storm, all the animals were silent, most likely safe inside their homes, right where she wanted to be.

With a heavy sigh, she looked down at her arm where the demon had grabbed her and frowned. There were two deep gashes cut across her bicep. The demon's claws must have torn the skin when she kicked him and yanked out of his grasp. She shifted her gaze to the cuff around her wrist, which was similar to the one they'd picked up last month from their fight with the demons in Georgia. The same kind the fiends had tried to put around her sister's wrist to take her; a ploy of Kalissa's psycho ex-boyfriend.

Khloe knew from personal experience that the iron

in the bracelet would keep her wound from healing since the ability to heal herself came from the magic in her blood. In fact, the scratches were starting to redden around the edges and would become infected if she didn't get somewhere to clean them.

A rumble across the sky brought her head up. The storm was closer. She needed to find shelter soon and then figure out how to get the damned cuff off. She walked through the brush and trees, not sure where she was or where to go.

"How do you get into these predicaments, Khloe?" She scolded herself as she proceeded forward. "Always in trouble." But, this time, no one knew where she was.

She continued to walk, searching for something she could use as shelter. She froze when that warm shiver fluttered across her skin again. Her not-so-secret admirer was near. Too near. Something brushed against her aura, and she whirled around in time to see the translucent outline of a shadow. Her heart stopped briefly then kicked into overdrive. She twisted to her left and ran.

Swatting at the low tree limbs, she ran as fast as her legs could go and went deeper into the forest. She jumped over a fallen tree trunk, ignoring the slaps from the low branches of tree saplings and brush on her legs and arms. The dark, warm, sensual energy caressing her back told her it was the large demon who had killed the ones that had chased her.

She took a sharp right and willed her legs to run

faster. They were starting to burn. She was not used to mere mortal strength.

Fucking cuff.

Her foot caught on something, and she went down. Twisting to the side to keep from landing face-first in the dirt, she fell on her left knee and side as she hit the ground. She hissed as pain shot through her leg up to her hip.

Almost instantly, the demon appeared, standing over her. He was huge and gorgeous, peering down at her with a not-so-pleasant expression. His black, shoulder-length hair hung in his face as he stared down at her, his chest rising and falling with each breath. Fear churned in her belly, and she scooted backward on her bottom away from him. She picked up a handful of dirt and threw it at him. When she tried to get up again, her knee hurt so bad she cried out and fell back down on her ass. *Now you've done it.*

He knelt down in front of her. "I will not harm you."

Want some candy, little girl? She cringed and began crab-crawling away from him. He stood. She took the opportunity to try to rise again. Relieved when she made it to her feet, she hobbled off in the opposite direction from where he stood. Suddenly, he appeared in front of her again. She let out a squeak and took a hop backward on her good leg.

Trapped and injured.

Wonderful.

It was bad enough that her arm was still bleeding

and hurt like hell. Now, her knee had started to swell. To top it off, she was powerless. How did humans do it? Right, they were born without magic.

And, they didn't have demons chasing them.

A rustle of leaves to her left sent a wave of panic through her. Why couldn't this be the day they took Teddy-Bear to the dog park? At least with the hell-hounds, she'd have a chance against the determined demons chasing her.

A rumble, followed by a flash of lightning in the sky made her flinch. "Shit." She breathed out. A snap of a twig followed by a dark power gliding over her skin gave her chills. Something large was coming.

"You're better off with me." The husky voice was too close for her comfort.

"What is it?" she whispered, looking back at the sound of footsteps growing closer.

"Demons." She looked up at his face. He sniffed the air. "Three *Regals*." He reached out and grabbed her left bicep. She groaned in pain. He frowned and roughly turned her arm over. "It's not healing," he stated.

"You think?" Khloe pulled from his grip, limping around him. At least she was able to walk, although, she wasn't sure for how long, and running was not an option with her knee the way it was. "What do we do?" She held up her wrist with the cuff around it. "No magic." She couldn't face *Regals* without her magic. She was as good as dead.

He held out his hand, palm up. "You can trust me, Khloe."

She looked into his chocolate-brown eyes for several moments. Tiny rivers of red flowed and twisted around the pupils. Could she trust a demon who looked so damn good?

Hell, no.

She was sure it would be a mistake, but what other option did she have? If he wanted her dead, he wouldn't be standing in front of her, waiting for her decision. Gods, she hoped she wasn't making the biggest mistake of her life. She raised her hand and placed it in his.

The forest faded out around her. She'd never been on the receiving end of teleportation. With her own magic, it was familiar, and she was in control. With this demon doing the teleporting, it was like she was being pulled through thick air at a rapid speed.

They took form in a bedroom, Khloe realized with a scowl. He noticed and gave her a sideways grin. *Arrogant ass. Laugh it up, demon.*

She looked around the room. "Where are we?"

"There's a shower through there." He pointed to the door on the left. "Don't leave the room." Then he exited, closing the door behind him.

Khloe stood there, staring at the door as if she could will it back open. He had her thoroughly confused. He was a demon, a very powerful one at that. She could feel his power even with her magic muted. Yet, he was different. Almost god-like. There was concern in that smooth voice that caressed her skin every time he spoke.

However, he had ordered her to stay put. She frowned in annoyance. *Who does he think he is?* No one ordered Khloe around. Not even her sister. Even her parents had had a hard time in that department while she was growing up.

That last thought brought back unwanted sorrow. The demons had killed them.

She pulled the cell phone out of her back pocket and noticed the screen was broken. Using the power button, she cursed softly. The whole phone was broken. Awesome!

She looked around for a landline and found nothing. Disappointment added to her growing irritation with the demon. *Damnit.* Kalissa must be pacing the floor with worry and giving everyone an earful.

However, Khloe doubted it would help matters if she contacted her sister. She wasn't sure where she was. She did know she wasn't in the natural world anymore. The air in the room told her that. It was lighter, in a magical, positive energy kind of way.

Deciding to wait until she got back home, she turned from the door and wondered if the demon could be trusted. He claimed to be there to help keep her safe. *Nope.* The ones that made such claims usually turned out to be the real monsters. She'd have to keep an eye on him.

With a heavy sigh, she hobbled into the bathroom and smiled at the promise of being clean after her romp through the forest.

Samoan grew more impatient the longer she stood watching the witch stare at the stone. Seriously. How long did it take to transfer power into a crystal?

"Hurry up, witch."

The witch slammed the gemstone on the stainless steel table and turned to lock gazes with Samoan. Ice-blue eyes framed by a slightly rounded face offered a challenge she was more than happy to accept.

"I told you before that I can't activate it. It's an uncharged piece of the Sinew."

Not buying it, Samoan pressed harder. "You're a Divinity. Now finish it."

"I'm a soul-keeper, not a goddess."

Samoan counted to three. If they didn't need the witch for information, she'd strike her down for the snotty tone and that eye roll.

Bitch.

"What does that mean exactly?"

The witch's shoulders tensed. At first, Samoan didn't think she'd answer. Samoan was about to loosen the little bitch's tongue, but she turned, lifted her chin, and replied. "I'm a *Porter*."

Fuck me. There was no way she was a guardian of lost souls. "*Porters* don't exist anymore. They were all killed thousands of years ago."

Another eye roll from the way-too-cocky Divinity hit another nerve. "All the full-blooded *Porters* died over three thousand years ago. The bloodline continues through other species."

Samoan filed away this new intel for later. Her mission, at the moment, was to activate the crystal into a copy of the Sinew—the source of all magic. "So, Miss Smarty, if you can't do it, then who can?"

The strawberry-blonde cocked her head and smiled. "Hecate."

Before she could control her instincts, Samoan backhanded the bitch hard enough that the witch stumbled back against the table. The witch pulled herself to a stand. Wiping her mouth with the back of her hand and peering down at the blood, a smile raised one corner of her lips in a sideways smirk, and she charged at Samoan.

Samoan found herself flat on her back with the witch straddling her. Hands wrapped tightly around her throat. Her lungs struggled to draw in air. Coldness crawled up her arms then wrapped around her spine as pain ripped through her chest. The witch's eyes grew darker, almost a midnight blue. Swirls of silver spiraled around the pupils. Then Samoan felt it—her soul began to rise from her body.

Fuck. She wasn't bluffing about being a Porter.

Samoan coughed. "If…I die…your son…dies."

The tearing pain stopped. The sense of her soul slamming back into her body replaced the numb, hollow feeling she'd experienced. Samoan gasped for air. She stared at the *Porter* for several seconds before an iron cuff slapped around the witch's wrist, and she was yanked off Samoan.

Pulling herself upright, Samoan leaned against a chair and glared at the *Porter*. "Take her out of my sight," she barked to the *Lackey* holding the soul-stealing Divinity.

She would definitely have to find a way to mute the soul keeper's power and find out how many more there were out there. An army of them could be useful.

CHAPTER FOUR

"What are you up to?"

Jagger groaned at the sound of his brother's voice behind him. He closed his eyes and drew in a deep breath. He so didn't need to fight with Lex right now.

"My job." He turned and walked past Lex to the other side of the study where a set of drawers lined the opposite wall next to a bookshelf.

"Your job…"

"Is to protect them," Jagger said through clenched teeth as he whirled around to stand nose to nose with Lex.

Lex smirked. "From a distance, brother."

Jagger turned back to search the contents of the drawers. "I had no choice." He sighed and lowered his shoulders. He gave Lex the short version of the attack on the Divinities and Khloe's self-sacrifice to keep the others safe. "I had to get her out of there. I'd have no problem taking on the *Regals*, but with her powers muted, she'd be nothing but a distraction."

A silver key appeared in front of his face. Jagger wrapped his fingers around it, but Lex held onto the ring connected to it. "What are your motives? And don't think about brushing this off as an 'I'm doing my job' bit. I know you." He paused, searching Jagger's face, then smiled. "You like the female."

Figures. One of the rare occasions Jagger saw any kind of emotion on his brother's face, and it was at his expense. "I believe now, more than ever, that Khan has some kind of power source. The demons are growing stronger. They are targeting the Divinities one at a time."

"This is not new news."

Snatching the key out of Lex's hand, Jagger growled and turned toward the door. He stopped when his brother asked, "What can I do to help?"

"Can you go keep a watch on the Divinity House?" he asked over his shoulder. Lex gave a short nod. Relief rolled through Jagger. "Thanks." He rushed out of the study and back upstairs where he'd left Khloe.

When he arrived at his bedroom door, he paused and listened. It was quiet except for her heartbeat. By the rapid rate, he could tell she was frustrated. Smiling, he twisted the knob and slowly pushed open the door.

She sat on the bed with her head bent, picking at the lock on the cuff until he stepped inside the room and shut the door with a soft click. Her head snapped up, her eyes a darker teal than they'd been when he'd left her. Stunned, he stared as if seeing her for the first time. Her face was clean of makeup, showing her natural beauty, but it was her hair that caught his attention. Wet from the shower, it cascaded over her shoulders. The pink streaks were gone. He shifted his eyes to her attire. She wore nothing but an oversized bath towel wrapped around her small frame, tucked in between her breasts to hold it in place.

The only things that remained the same were her tiny nose piercing and a small hoop through her eyebrow.

"What?" she snapped.

Blinking, he closed the door and walked toward her. He held out the key to the cuff she'd been trying to open when he came in. She hesitantly reached out and took it, then eagerly slid the key into the lock and turned it. When the cuff fell free, she closed her eyes and inhaled deeply. Jagger knew she needed her elements soon to draw in more strength, but first, he wanted her to rest.

"Why were you staring at me when you came in?" she said after a few brief moments. There was mistrust in her tone. The way she kept her distance from him, he would bet she didn't allow many people inside the wall she'd built around herself.

He smiled at her. "I was admiring your beauty."

Khloe scrunched up her face and rolled her eyes. "I

doubt that. You were admiring a half-naked woman sitting on your bed."

That made his smile widen. Normally, it would anger him to have someone speak to him in such a way, but there was something different about the female in front of him.

"And that," he teased and walked into the bathroom.

The mixture of their scents slammed into him, making him take a step back. It was an exotic aroma of spiced hot chocolate. She'd used his soap. He knew she would, but he was not prepared for the effect it would have on him. It took everything he had not to turn around and claim her. Possess every inch of her.

He'd been charged with keeping her safe from the demons. But who was going to keep her safe from him?

The rush of unbound power ran through her veins. It was wonderful to have her magic back online. Khloe was so grateful, she could have kissed the demon, but he turned to go into the bathroom.

She eyed the doorway. He had been in there for a

while. She was tempted to ask if he'd fallen in, but the door was still open. Stepping to the side just enough to peek inside, she saw his reflection in the mirror. He was pulling items out of a drawer, then he opened the medicine cabinet. With a sigh, she turned to the bedroom door, wondering if she would be able to make a run for it. Not a chance. He would track her down. Besides, she didn't even know where she was.

Giving up on the hope for escape, she looked down at her wound and frowned. It was still sore and red. *Odd.* Her magic should have healed it, or at least started to heal it.

She conjured clothes onto her body and sighed at the feeling of a fresh pair of jeans and a soft tank top. Might as well be comfortable.

"Why did you do that?"

Startled, she whirled around toward the sound of Jagger's voice as he emerged from the bathroom. She studied him, suspicious of his meaning and still unsure why he'd brought her to his home. "Do what? Get dressed?"

The conflicting emotions that ran across his face almost made her laugh out loud. He sobered quickly and said, "Your hair."

"Oh." She shrugged.

"Why do you use glamour to hide your natural beauty?"

She looked straight at him. Had he just called her beautiful? "Am I not pretty now?" Again with the debatable look. He opened his mouth then closed it again. "I don't cover up my looks. I alter them. You try growing up looking identical to someone else." She rolled her eyes.

"I have."

She searched his face for a few moments. "You're a twin?"

Shaking his head, he walked to her, motioning to the bed. She sat back down, not taking her eyes off him. "I have a brother. We are not twins, but we looked so much alike when we were younger, that we were often mistaken as being identical."

"That didn't bother you?" she asked.

He sat down on the bed so that he faced her. "Why should it? You and Kalissa may look alike, but you are different. Your eyes are different colors," he pointed out.

"True. But I like being different." She winced when he took her injured arm in his large, firm grasp.

"Infection is starting to set in. This will help." He opened an amber-colored jar and scooped out a small amount of the cream with his fingertips. The smell of willow bark, lavender, and rosemary drifted up from the creamy mixture. She flinched as the cool cream touched her cut. His eyes flicked up to meet hers, concern heavy in his gaze. "Does that hurt?"

She shook her head. "No. It's just cold." One side of his mouth lifted in a smile of amusement. "I don't understand why my magic hasn't sped up the healing process."

"The infection could have started before the cuff was removed. It will take a little while for your magic to repair everything."

Watching as he carefully and tenderly spread the cream over her wound, she wondered who and what he was. "What's your name?"

"Jagger."

"What are you?"

He didn't look at her as he answered, "Death Demon."

Those two words should have scared the shit out of her, but they didn't. In fact, they made her want to know more about the sensual creature sitting in front of her who was so cautiously tending to her wound. She also wanted to better understand the amount of power he possessed. Death Demons were the strongest of the demonic race, and most served the gods.

As if feeling her inquisition, he lifted his chocolate-brown eyes. "I'm tied to Hecate."

He offered his left arm to her, palm up, revealing Hecate's Wheel perfectly etched on the inside of his wrist. It was identical to the one she'd received during Kalissa and Ayden's binding ceremony. She reached out to touch his mark, but he pulled his arm away before her fingers made contact. If he worked under Hecate's command, he was on her side.

That still didn't mean she could trust him.

After tightening the lid, he shifted to set the jar of cream on the bed between them and picked up the roll of bandages. In times like these, she wished she were empathic like Zach, or better yet, telepathic. She'd love to know what the demon was thinking.

He was truly a beautiful creature with his jet-black hair, honey-tanned skin, and strong jawline. But, he carried that dark, dangerous essence that all demons possessed. He might pledge his loyalty to Hecate, but what was keeping him from turning on her, on everyone she loved?

Khloe had always fallen too fast for men. A handsome face and nice words had gotten her heart broken enough times to harden it a bit. She would defiantly keep an eye on the demon, especially where her heart was concerned. That door was locked, deadbolted, and chained. There was no getting in. She'd made that mistake five years ago. Mark had turned on her, and he was human. She wasn't about to watch history repeat itself.

"So. What's next?" she asked, not taking her eyes off his face.

He finished dressing her wound, tying off the bandage to secure it in place and stood to put everything away. "You need to rest, build your strength. When you wake, I'll take you outside."

Where's the damn leash? She narrowed her eyes at him. "I am capable of walking myself."

He moved so fast she didn't have time to blink

before he was inches from her face. "You will do as I say. This is my home," he growled and then turned and left the room.

Jagger was still fuming about Khloe's defiant tone when he reached his mother's chambers. The female brought too many emotions to the surface; lust being the leader, followed by possessiveness and heartache.

With a deep breath, he pushed away the dull tightness in his chest before entering the room without knocking. What was the use when the goddess knew he was coming?

"Mother?" he called, not seeing her inside the entryway of her private quarters, which was more like a small suite, consisting of a living room with a loveseat and two armchairs as well as a bedroom with en-suite bathroom. He walked toward her bedroom.

Once inside, he saw her standing in front of the window on the right side of the room. Her long, midnight-black hair hung loosely down her back and encircled her shoulders. She wore a white gown that blended with her porcelain skin and was the perfect contrast to her dark hair.

She turned to face him as he entered the room and frowned. She was annoyed with him. He knew that annoyance all too well. "You were not to make contact with any of them."

He closed his eyes, holding his irritation in check. "I felt I had no choice."

"We all have choices, Jag." She walked to sit in the chair at her vanity.

"I don't understand the logic behind why we can't make contact. We are to help them." He moved to the window and peered out across the garden. Under the dim light of the moon, multi-colored streamers trailed behind the pixies as they played among the roses. He wondered if Khloe would like to see the gardens. Thinking she might, he decided it would be the first place he took her in the morning.

The sound of a hairbrush touching the dresser a little harder than it should, brought his attention back to the goddess, who was studying him in her mirror. He cleared his head of thoughts of the little distraction in his bedroom, sleeping in his bed...

"She was injured, and the demons were upon us. Her powers were bound." He didn't need to explain himself. Hecate knew, but she wouldn't let him leave without hearing his side. She was the Goddess of Witchcraft, and the witches were hers to guide and protect. She knew what they did, their thoughts, and their prayers. With the war against the demons upon them, she kept a closer watch on her witches and the rest of *magickin*.

"But you revealed yourself. Went against a direct order." He fell silent because there was no use explaining it. She sighed heavily. "Zeus will not grant them more powers than they already have. He also refuses to get involved with my witches and has forbidden me from helping them directly. I can guide them, but not fight with them. He was put off that I created the Divinities in the first place." The goddess rolled her eyes and turned to Jagger. "Hades is no help. He denies knowing anything about Khan's plan or his whereabouts. I think for once in his life, he's siding with his brother."

Jagger nodded. They were on their own in the war. The gods had shut them out. Like the Fates did him and Lex so long ago when they'd allowed their people to die.

"Khloe is a free spirit and has no fear when it comes to this war. That is why I assigned you and Lex to them as their guardians. You carry too much of my power and scent on you. If the other demons caught your scent—"

"They were confused by it," he interrupted. She glared at him and raised a brow. "In the forest, I could mask my and her scent. It worked to distract them."

"But, they found you."

He nodded. "I'm not sure why they were able to track her."

"And you panicked and brought her here?" Hecate looked at him, no expression on her face.

He hung his head and spoke softly. "It was the only place I thought would be safe for her to heal."

The goddess was silent for several minutes before speaking. "What is done is done. You finish this mission you are on. Khloe is yours to deal with."

His heart skipped a couple of beats, unsure if he liked her amused tone. "Yes, Mother." He turned to walk out of the room.

When he reached his own room again, he found Khloe curled up on his bed, asleep. He stood over her, watching her rest peacefully for a few moments before taking a deep breath and moving to the other side of the bed. He sat down on top of the covers next to her and watched the rise and fall of her chest as she slept. He withdrew a leather-bound journal from the nightstand drawer and tried to push Hecate's words from his mind.

Khloe is yours to deal with.

CHAPTER FIVE

Khloe woke the next morning enveloped in warmth that smelled earthy and spicy with a hint of sandalwood, but there was another scent. It was vaguely familiar, yet she couldn't place where she'd picked it up before. With her eyes still closed, she snuggled into the warmth and breathed in the wonderful smells. It reminded her of Willow's scent when she returned from the Afterworld.

Alarmed, she flung her eyes open and scrambled backward off the bed. The Death Demon had taken it upon himself to share the bed with her. The creep was sound asleep as if he belonged there. Okay, so it was his bed, but she hadn't given him permission to be there with her.

"Wake up!" she demanded, throwing her pillow at him.

Jagger jolted awake, sitting straight up. "What? What's wrong?"

"You," she blurted out with her hands on her hips. "What do you think you're doing?"

He gave her a confused, sleepy-eyed expression that quickly changed to amusement, like her distress was funny.

"Wipe that smug look off your face," she fumed.

With smirk intact, he swung his feet to the floor, stood, and stalked around the bed toward her. She swallowed hard and hated the desire that raced through her veins like lava. The tiny flame inside her, the piece of her that belonged to the element of Fire, ignited and intensified at the feel of his aura. Her sex ached, begging to be touched by him. He was gorgeous —the hard, lean muscles of his bare shoulders flexing and rolling as he prowled closer. She let her gaze roam over his body as he advanced closer to her in nothing but his boxer-briefs. She swallowed hard and lifted her gaze back to his face. Logic told her to run, but her body said, "bring it." It had been way too long...

How could this demon have such an effect on her?

"Don't come any closer," she whispered.

"Why not, Khloe?" It was a growl, and gods, it sent that hot, lusty need straight to her sex. He stopped about six inches from her. "Why are you angry?"

"You never said you would be sleeping in the bed with me." She lifted her chin, proud that her tone was firm.

The smirk turned into a smile. Damn, did he even realize the effect his smile had on a woman? He probably did. He was male, after all.

"I never said I wasn't." She opened her mouth and then closed it when he continued, "Did I not sleep on top of the covers?" he purred.

Her eyes shifted to the side of the bed where he'd slept. The covers were pulled up, just as it had been when she'd gotten there. Nodding, she looked back at him. "I just...panicked."

"Get dressed. We're going for a walk."

"Why?" she said, not holding back the suspicion in her tone.

"Are you always so mistrusting?" he said, lifting a brow.

"When my escort is a demon, yes." She willed on a pair of jeans and a T-shirt to replace her nightgown. She was glad she'd conjured her long gown to sleep in as opposed to one of her small babydolls.

His eyes roamed over her body, making her uncomfortably aroused. Then, in a blink, his clothes changed to a black T-shirt and jeans. He held out his hand to her. "Shall we?"

Ignoring his outstretched palm, Khloe shoved past him to the bedroom door and opened it. She stiffened when he leaned into her and said, "Follow me." His warm breath against her skin made her shudder. He let out a soft chuckle as he walked around her to lead the way.

Once outside, she followed him down a small path around the massive house. He glanced back several times. Probably making sure she didn't run off. But, seriously, where would she go?

Watching her footsteps instead of Jagger's yummy backside, she didn't notice when he stopped, and she ran right into his hard back. She let out a soft curse. He held his hand up for silence. She was about to tell him where he could stick that hand, when two pixies zipped by, halting her verbal outburst.

She stepped around Jagger and gasped at the beautiful gardens that stretched on as far as she could see. Pixies zigzagged from the roses to the cherry trees, leaving trails of brightly colored pixie dust behind them.

"Incredible. There are pixies at the coven, but I've never seen so many in one place." She pushed past him to walk farther into the gardens.

"They love the gardens. Plus, they are well protected here."

Glancing back to see his expression, she caught movement in one of the second-floor windows of the house. A woman peered down at them, and Khloe knew instantly who she was. The bond to the goddess alone told her.

Shifting her gaze to meet Jagger's, she asked, "You live with Hecate?"

He didn't answer. Instead, he glanced to the

window then back to her, a frown forming on his handsome face. "Let's go down to the river."

Mood lifting at the thought of being near a natural body of water, she hopped into step with him when he started to stroll down the path.

A few feet away from the gardens, the trail opened to a small clearing with a view of the river. "Wow, it's beautiful."

He stepped aside. "I thought you might like it here," he said as she walked past him, admiring her surroundings. Inside the small clearing, encircled by large weeping willows, she was in awe of how vibrant everything appeared. The grass was so green it looked painted. The trees and other plants radiated life. Closing her eyes, she breathed in the vibrancy around her, thanking the goddess for her blessings.

"It's beautiful," she repeated, kicking off her shoes and rolling up her pant legs.

She sat on the edge of the riverbank, placed her feet into the water, and listened. The water swiftly flowed around her feet, birds chirped happily in the distance, and tiny bells could be heard from across the narrow river. No, not bells. That was the laughter of the pixies.

"This is one of my favorite spots," Jagger revealed.

She looked at his large frame, casually leaning against a tree. "It's peaceful. Magical."

"This is a magical realm," he replied.

She gave a short nod and turned her head to peer out into the forest across the river. After several minutes, no longer able to stand his eyes on her, she asked, "You gonna stand there and stare at me all day?"

"I might." His tone had a smile in it.

She stood up, picked up her shoes, and walked over to stand in front of him. "When can I go home?"

"When you are stronger, we will return to the human world."

"When can I go *home*?" she asked again with hands on her hips.

He dropped his shoulders. "As soon as I figure out why they need your powers."

Her eyes narrowed. "What about my powers?"

"The demons that chased you wanted your and Kalissa's powers. So, until I find out why, the two of you need to stay separated."

Khloe pursed her lips. "Until then?"

"You're stuck with me," he informed her with a wide grin.

"That's nice," she said wryly and then threw her hands up and walked away.

Back at the house a few hours later, Khloe sat at the kitchen table eating lunch. Jagger had warmed up a bowl of vegetable soup and made a turkey sandwich for her and then he'd left. The Death Demon irritated the hell out of her, and yet, he ignited her senses. He confused her. He was a fierce creature with the ability to kill with only a thought. He was bossy, seemingly possessive, and stubborn. Yet, he had been concerned and tender while dressing her wound, and at ease during their walk.

The air pressure in the room changed, making a crooked grin pull at her lips. "I know you're here." She took the last piece of crust from her sandwich and soaked up the remnants of her soup before popping it into her mouth.

Jagger materialized beside her. "How are you feeling?"

"Much better. The little outing helped a lot," she said, shifting her gaze to his face. She felt great actually. Almost completely recharged. She'd gathered what energy she could from the elements outside—all except for Fire. That side of her ran off her passion, meaning one sure way to fully recharge was sexual release, something she would have to take care of once she got home because she sure wasn't going to sleep with the Death Demon.

"When are you taking me home?"

He picked up her plate and carried it to the sink. "We're not going yet."

Annoyed, she drew her eyebrows together. "What? Why?" She wanted to go now. Together, the Divinities could find out what the demons were up to and stop them.

"Because it's safer for everyone that way."

He came back and held out his hand to her. She stubbornly folded her arms over her chest and glared. "That's not an answer."

"Demons want your powers. They want to use you for whatever plot they have brewing."

She didn't like his tone.

"I'm not a child!" She jerked away as he reached to take her arm. "I can take care of myself. Take me home. Now!"

Pivoting on her heel, she turned to leave the kitchen. She had to get away from the bossy-ass demon. His commands irritated her to the point of madness.

She got as far as the kitchen door before her back was pressed against the wall, held in place by Jagger. The rivers of red swirling in his chocolate eyes brightened and glowed. His erection pressed against her stomach, telling her he was far from angry. She parted her lips to protest the sudden invasion of her personal space, but the words died on her tongue as his mouth covered hers. She moaned, met his demanding assault, and moved her hips against him. His spicy earth scent filled her head, making her dizzy with need. Her blood boiled, and her heart danced, skipping beats. Her earlier anger dissolved into waves of desire and lust. The Fire inside her stirred and encouraged her to take what he was offering.

He broke the kiss to say, "I was sent to protect you. You will do as I say." Then he vanished.

She sagged against the wall, finding it hard to breathe. It wasn't from fear. Gods, she hadn't been that turned on in years. If that was her punishment, she was going to be lippy more often.

Snap out of it, girl.

With a deep breath, she pushed away from the wall to search for him. She wasn't done with their conversation.

CHAPTER SIX

*J*agger stepped out of the ice-cold shower and groaned. Khloe was near. He felt her presence. Smelled her alluring scent. Hands pressed flat on the black marble counter, he stared at his reflection. His eyes no longer glowed from the intense passion of the kiss.

Damn it! Why had he touched her?

Because she raised emotions within him that no other had. No other *dared*. Her annoyance and anger fueled him. When she demanded to be taken home, he'd lost it, his voice of reason squashed like a bug flying head-on into a car windshield at eighty miles per hour.

The kiss had been a mistake.

Call Lex. Put him in charge of the female.

It was the smartest thing to do. But the mere thought of her near another male drove his already edgy mood into lethal territory. Even his brother wasn't safe.

There was a soft tap on the bathroom door. He said nothing.

"Jagger?" Khloe moved away from the doorway and muttered a curse.

He closed his eyes. He was too wound up to argue with her.

"Look. I get it. I can't go home and endanger the others. We can go to my condo. It's familiar and close to Kalissa and the others. Besides, we can't leave them in the dark regarding what is going on. They're as much a part of this war as we are." She fell silent. Her footsteps indicating that she'd walked away from the door once more.

A smile tugged at his lips as her words sank in. He opened the door. "You're homesick."

She whirled around from the window and looked at him offensively. "Am not."

His smirk turned into a frown. He crossed the room in an instant. She was still weak, and he didn't understand why. In the magical realm of the Afterworld, she should have healed almost completely in the twenty-four hours they'd been there. He took her arm and turned it over to peer at the wound. It had closed up, but it had not healed. He lifted his eyes to her teal gaze then lowered to her lips, still slightly swollen from the kiss. He dropped her arm and stepped back, his frown deepening.

"What is it?"

"You're not at full power."

She glared at him, placing her hands on her hips in irritation. "And your point?"

"Do you know why?"

She turned away from him. "Maybe it has something to do with being here, away from my twin."

Shit. She was right.

Before he could respond, she asked, "What about my family? Are they safe?"

"Yes. My brother, Lex, is watching over the house." He paused then reached out but dropped his hand. "Give me twenty-four hours. I need to figure out what the demons are up to."

She turned from the window to peer at him. "We can do that at home with my family."

He had never met a more stubborn female in his existence. With a growl, he stepped into her space. "There is someone I must see first."

Straightening her spine and narrowing her eyes, she stood her ground. "And who would that be?"

He took a step back and turned away before he did something stupid. Like, kiss her again.

He stepped into the closet and grabbed a leather jacket. When he exited the small walk-in, Khloe stood where he'd left her with her arms crossed, irritation heavy in both her scent and her expression. He handed her the jacket. "An Oracle just outside the Darklands."

"Why?"

He clenched his teeth and silently counted. Must she know everything? Question everything? "She owes me a favor." Thrusting the jacket into her arms, he pivoted and left the room.

Halfway down the stairs, he heard her footsteps closing in on him. He didn't dare look at her. He didn't want to see her in his jacket. The smell of leather mixed with both their scents was driving him crazy enough. Falling into step with him, she remained silent. Most likely plotting something in that inquisitive mind of hers.

Outside, he led her to a small garage a few feet away from the main house. He opened the double doors to reveal his only earthly possession: a 1930 Harley.

"Wow." She glided forward to run her fingers over the handlebars. "It's in perfect condition." Meeting his gaze, she smiled. "Did you buy it brand new?"

He chuckled at her teasing tone and shook his head. "No, Lex did." He picked up the helmet from the seat and handed it to her. "Put this on."

She wrinkled her nose, and damn if his cock didn't twitch. "What about you?"

"I've been told I have a hard head." Amusement lit up her face, but she looked away as if hiding it. "Besides, my chances of surviving a crash are a hundred times better than yours."

When she took the helmet and placed it on her head, he swung his leg over the bike, sat, and fired her up. Moments later, she was seated behind him, arms wrapped around his waist, and they were riding down a dirt road towards the Darklands.

Jagger pulled off the road, turned off the bike, and waited for Khloe to dismount before he did. Pushing the bike into an opening in the brush, he touched the nearest vine. In seconds, the whole area was covered with them, hiding the cycle from sight.

"Your ruling element is Earth?"

He nodded. "And Fire."

"I didn't know demons could control the elements."

He held out his hand to her and wasn't surprised when she didn't take it. "They can't. And I'm not a regular demon."

She followed him to the path that led to the village. "What does that mean?"

"From the beginning of time, the Death Demons have served the gods. Many mated with them and their descendants."

"So, you're like a demi-god?"

"In some ways." He stopped and turned to face her. "Must you ask so many questions?"

She shrugged. "It's the only way to find things out. Is Hecate your mother?"

"She is my adoptive mother. She took Lex and me in after our village was destroyed."

"Which god are you descended from?"

Shaking his head, he continued down the footpath. "My biological mother was one of the Fates."

"Which one?"

"Don't know. Don't care." He peered at her from the corner of his eye and sighed. "The Fates took my family from me. I want nothing to do with them."

She fell silent and didn't ask another question the rest of the walk to the village. He welcomed the lack of conversation and the chance to think. He was surprised how much of himself he had revealed to her in such a short period.

"Welcome to Felicity," he announced as they walked through the opened gates.

Khloe was speechless. The village was similar to the Maxville Coven. As they walked along the edge of the cobblestone road, the only difference she noticed was that there were shops and a school among the many cottages.

"It's beautiful."

"Why, thank you."

Khloe turned toward the soft voice. Shock stole her voice again. The woman standing in front of her was an elf. Her pointed ears peeked out from behind white-blond hair that fell to her ankles. She wore a blue gown much like the ones Willow loved to wear.

"Lo!"

Turning at the familiar voice, Khloe faced her adopted sister, the wood nymph that lived near their cabin in the Blue Ridge Mountains. "Willow?"

She flew toward Khloe, hugging her so tightly it was hard to breathe. "Why are you here? How did you get here?" Stepping back, she noticed Jagger. "Oh, I see." She nodded to the demon with a frown. "Jagger."

"Nice to see you again, Willow."

"Yeah, yeah. You come to see Clara?" When he didn't answer or move, Willow tsked. "I know you did. She said you were coming. Now go. Shoo. I'll take care of Lo."

It was several moments before Jagger released a low growl and left.

"You have got to tell me how you did that."

Willow laughed and looped her arm with Khloe's to

tug her toward a large building. "He's your guardian, not mine."

Khloe frowned. She hadn't asked for a guardian, nor did she want one. Especially the sexy and irritating Death Demon. "Where are we going?"

Mischief crept into Willow's pale green eyes. "You'll see, my ever-so-curious Lo."

Khloe smiled and quickly relaxed. Having someone she knew and loved beside her was comforting. "You know I hate being out of my element."

"Yes, I know, but you can trust Jagger."

Khloe nodded but didn't comment. Sure, Jagger seemed loyal, and she had seen a small part of his softer side, but she wouldn't be handing her heart over to him anytime soon, if ever. That would be too easy for her to do. He ignited something inside her, the same something that made her fall for the wrong men for the wrong reasons.

Entering the building that she now recognized as a community center of some sort, she was met by chattering youngsters sitting in the middle of the open-spaced floor. When the children saw them, they got up and ran over. "Who is she?" a tiny elf girl asked.

Another elfin, a boy who looked about seven, said, "She's a goddess."

That got all the children talking at once. Willow clapped her hands, silencing everyone. "She is not a goddess. But she is a very powerful witch."

A shower of "oohs" and "aahs" came from the

group. Willow squatted in front of them. "And guess what?"

"What?" The chorus of tiny voices made Khloe laugh.

"She's going to show you how to dance."

The group of little creatures jumped for joy and started talking all at once again.

"Willow, I don't—"

"Oh, come on. It'll be fun. Their teacher has fallen ill, and they need cheering up."

Khloe peered out at the faces of the adorable group of *magickin* children and sighed. "Okay, I'll do it."

"Yay!" the group sang out.

Thank the gods for small blessings.

Jagger would have to send Willow a gift for being here and entertaining Khloe. Somehow, he didn't think she would mix well with Clara.

He mounted the stairs of the main house in the village. It was the largest and served as the great hall of the community as well as Clara's home. Pure white, accented in crimson and gold, the small mansion fit the Oracle in every way possible.

The front door opened before he could knock. Clara's beautiful, smiling face greeted him. She leaned into him but stopped inches from his face. "Oh. For once, I didn't see this. You have met your mate."

He nodded, knowing better than to lie to an Oracle.

Her smile widened, and she shifted to kiss him on the cheek instead of the usual soft peck on the lips she'd greeted him with in past meetings. It was rumored that her mother was a succubus, and the power of seduction had been passed down to her. Jagger didn't know how true those tales were, but he suspected there was some truth to them. He had never had the balls to ask either. That was her personal business.

"You know why I have come."

"Yes. Please sit."

He did, and she sat across from him in an armchair. She studied him for several moments before dropping her shoulders. "I'm sorry. I can't see anything you don't already know."

"Are you sure?"

"Yes. However, I do know that this will not be an easy journey for either of you."

He stood and offered her his hand. She took it and allowed him to pull her to her feet. "Thanks, as always." He placed a palm-size ruby in her free hand.

Gasping, she shook her head. "This belonged to your birth mother."

"I want you to have it as payment for all the help over the years."

Her crystal gaze filled with tears, and she closed her hand around the gemstone and cradled it to her heart. "You are too kind to my people." Her words faded into a whisper, and her brows bunched together.

"What is it?" His stomach sank to his feet. Something in his soul told him he'd regret asking her.

Her eyes sparkled with silver as she stared back at him with a frown. "Your road ahead is bleak. I will not lie to you about that. You must open your heart to your love and seek your mother out."

When he jerked back from her, she gripped his hands with hers. Shaking his head, he said, "The Fates never cared to save my village. Why should I seek my mother out?"

"I feel strongly that you need to. I don't see why or how." Clara lowered her gaze and released his hands. "Be safe, Jagger."

Jagger stepped closer and pressed his lips to her forehead. "I will. Brightest blessings, Clara." He turned and walked out into the setting sun.

His future was bleak? What the hell did that mean? Did the Oracle see his death? Khloe's? He'd just have to be more aware of his surroundings and not let Khloe out of his sight. He'd be damned if he went to his mother for anything.

Loud music pounded from inside the community center when he reached the doors. Entering the stadium-sized building, he smiled. Khloe danced around the floor with ten small children, who giggled every time they missed a step.

He watched her drift around the floor as if she were made for dancing. Graceful and beautiful.

She spotted him and stopped. The music shut off instantly. Embarrassment coloring her face, she bent down to speak to the kids softly before she made her way to him.

"Why did you stop?"

She shrugged. It made him chuckle. Holding out his hand, he asked, "Are you ready to go home?"

CHAPTER SEVEN

They materialized a couple of feet from the high-rise condominiums along the St. John's River across from downtown Jacksonville, Florida. Khloe dropped Jagger's hand like a hot potato and ran for the door. Joy filled her at the promise of sleeping in a familiar bed, in her own room, with a door so she could lock the demon out.

The waterfront condos were her home away from home. Her sanctuary. The idea of bringing Jagger into her private space set her on edge. Kalissa had only been inside a couple of times since Khloe had purchased it five years before. After her breakup with Mark, she'd needed space to think, grieve, and release her rage in private.

Exiting the elevator into the foyer of her unit, she went straight for the phone in the living room. She lifted the receiver off the cradle and punched a button as she dropped into an oversized La-Z-Boy and swung her legs over the arm.

Jagger stood in front of her with a disapproving look. Whatever. She wrinkled her nose at him, which seemed to irritate him.

Good.

"Khloe? Thank the gods. Where are you?"

Her heart skipped several beats at the sound of Kalissa's frantic voice. "I'm safe. It is so good to hear your voice."

"When are you coming home?"

Khloe watched the demon shake his head. Figured he could hear both sides of the conversation. She waved him off and answered Kalissa's question, "Not sure right now. We need to figure this out."

"We?"

"Yeah. Our stalker..."

"Is a Death Demon." Kalissa finished her sentence.

"How did you know?"

"His brother showed up a couple of hours after Lydia and I got home."

"So he told you where I was?"

Kalissa said, "Yes."

Khloe quickly gave her sister the edited version of the past twenty-four hours.

"And he's there with you?" Lis didn't sound pleased.

Khloe shifted her eyes to Jagger, who had moved

toward the wall of nine-foot-tall windows that over-looked the river and downtown Jacksonville. "Yes, Death looms over me."

Her sister huffed, indicating she wasn't in the mood for Khloe's dry humor. Zach Manus, Maxville Deputy Sheriff and one of her best friends, would have come back with something.

"How is Zach coming along with surveillance?"

"He's not, really. The demons are keeping a low profile. I thought for sure the attack on us would bring them out. But, nothing. I can't even pick up anything on the radar. I've got a bad feeling about this." Kalissa's worried tone sent a sliver of fear through Khloe.

It was never good when the bad guys fell silent. They were plotting something. Khloe wanted to know what. Especially if those plans involved her. "If you hear anything, let us know. My phone broke, so I'll use my spare."

"Okay. Lo, be careful."

"I will. I love you."

"I love you, too. Talk to ya soon."

Khloe pressed the off button to the cordless and returned it to the base. She stood and went to the master suite. The first thing she was going to do was take a long, hot, invigorating shower. Dancing over to her dresser, she whipped open the drawer and picked out her sleepwear for the evening. When the air in the room shifted to that all-too-familiar but arousing demonic energy, she smirked inwardly and pulled out one of her babydoll nighties.

"Make yourself at home. I'm taking a shower." She walked past his large body, casually holding up her doorframe, into the bathroom, shutting and locking the door behind her.

Samoan Grayson prowled along the edge of the property, hidden within the forest, and sought out the prime opportunity to strike. The orange and pink glow of the sunset filtered in through the trees surrounding the coven.

The wards encompassing the small community were strong but only set to keep demons out. A grave mistake they would soon regret.

"What are you waiting for?" she growled into the ear of the Dark Divine that would get her inside the coven.

He squeezed his eyes shut as if her presence irritated him. Good. She wasn't here to please anyone.

"I'll let you know as soon as I find what I'm looking for." Movement to their right made him curse. "Damn it. Tell your demons to fall back. If they set off the wards, we're screwed."

With a flick of her hand, the impatient demons froze. "Anything else, Pete?"

He ignored her and continued stalking the outer edge of the perimeter, searching. "There." She followed his stare to two young adult, female Dark Divine hidden among the *magickin* that protected them.

"Is that them?" Samoan whispered in his ear. He shivered, and she smiled.

"Two of them." He shifted forward. After a few minutes, he said, "The other two are in that house."

Samoan nodded and gave the signal. The demons charged in as a single entity. Within seconds, the *magickin* males flooded out of their homes to defend their people.

Samoan grinned in satisfaction as her demon army attacked the village. Pete formed a basketball-sized fireball between his hands and thrust it toward the oncoming witches. Samoan joined in and threw two of her own—in different directions for good measure. Flames shot up into the sky and spread to consume anything in their path.

Pete teleported to snatch up the females, who had run toward the main house of the coven. Samoan flashed in and grabbed the two younger children from their slumbers. Coming out of the cabin, she noticed her *Lackeys* were getting their asses handed to them. She shook her head and decided to leave them. The lower demon class was expendable.

She gave Pete a short nod, and they dematerialized to take the Dark Divine children to their new homes.

CHAPTER EIGHT

A slow smile tugged at Jagger's lips as Khloe locked herself inside the bathroom to shower. Like a human-made lock could keep him out. Chuckling to himself, he stalked out of the bedroom to explore her home.

She didn't live here. The too-clean space told him that. He crossed the white marble floor to a set of French doors that opened to a balcony. The rest of the living room walls were lined with nine-foot-tall windows that revealed a beautiful view of the river and downtown Jacksonville. The orange and pink glow of the sunset lifted his lips in another smile. She'd chosen this unit for that view; he was sure.

The *swoosh* of the elevator door had him whirling around, ready to strike. His nostrils flared, and his eyes narrowed on the man stepping out of the lift. The male's golden gaze snapped up to meet Jagger's. A smirk had raised one side of the man's mouth before he turned toward the kitchen.

Zach Manus, the deputy sheriff of Maxville, and the witch who hung around Khloe a little too much to be healthy for him. Jagger's gaze followed the male as he set the paper bag he carried on the counter and opened the refrigerator.

"How did you get in?" Jagger scowled.

Zach pulled a container out of the icebox, opened it, and shuddered. Jagger's nose twitched at the rancid smell that lingered in the air.

"I have a key," Zach answered, throwing the rotten food in the trashcan.

Jagger clenched his jaw. Ask a stupid question, get a stupid answer. In this case, it was an obvious answer. "Why are you here?"

Amusement lit up the witch's face, then was replaced by mischief. "I came to see Lo."

Hand clenched at his side, Jagger forced himself to stay put and not choke the life out of the deputy. Watching the other male move around the kitchen as if he belonged there wasn't helping. But he did notice Zach's stiff movements and the way he watched Jagger from the corner of his eye. His aura turned a navy blue. Power surrounded him, and Jagger knew it had nothing to do with his dormant Divinity gene. There was something else hidden, almost as if a darker magic lurked within Zach.

Just as he opened his mouth, Khloe flew into the

room and tackled Zach in a tight hug. "Oh, my gods. What are you doing here? I mean, I didn't expect anyone to come over."

"Ayd said you were here, and I figured you needed some food." The witch's energy returned to his natural bright blue as he searched her face with concern.

She moved to the bag on the counter and peered inside. Jagger moved closer to take a look. When she lifted something out of the bag, she stepped back into him. Out of reflex, his hands gripped her hips, and he heard her sharp intake of breath. Jagger stole a quick glance at Zach, who had a look of amusement on his face, confirming that the empath had his shields down.

Khloe turned in Jagger's arms and stared into his eyes. With a palm flat on his chest, she pushed. A silent command to back off. That was when he noticed what she was wearing, or what she *wasn't* wearing. A low growl rumbled up his chest, and he took her by the upper arm and dragged her toward the bedroom.

Inside her room, Khloe snatched her arm out of the

demon's grasp and stabbed him with a stare. "What the fuck is your problem?"

"You," he growled, moving his eyes over her body.

She hated the sudden heat that formed in her belly and spread lower. With narrowed eyes, she studied him for a few seconds. A smile softened her anger, but only a little. He was jealous. How sweet.

But, seriously, that was Zach out there. It wasn't as if it were the hottie one floor below her. When she'd chosen her nightwear, she hadn't expected her BFF to stop by, or her protector to go into a jealous fit. She crossed her arms over her chest and looked up at her almost-seven-foot-tall demon. "How am I your problem?"

He opened his mouth and closed it again. Gods, she wanted to have that mouth on her, possessing every inch. And the next instant...it was. She wasn't sure if he'd read her mind or if she'd actually said the words aloud.

The bedroom door slammed shut, and she found herself being herded backward. She wrapped her arms around Jagger's neck and fisted his black hair. He moaned deep in his throat, and his tongue thrust into her mouth, finding hers.

Big hands slid to her ass and lifted her off the ground. She wrapped her legs around his waist and ground against his thick erection.

Her back touched the cool silk of the king-sized bedspread, and Jagger's mouth left hers. A moment later, his lips touched her right breast. She cried out at the sensation of his hot tongue flicking over her nipple.

A tap on the door froze them in place. Jagger lifted his gaze to hers, and she almost gasped. His eyes glowed pure red. Zach's voice drifted through the door.

"Um... I hate to be a party crasher, but the Oceanway Coven was just attacked."

The passion drained from Jagger's face, replaced by the hard, lethal expression he'd had yesterday when he killed the demons that had chased her from the mall. She was sure her own expression mirrored his.

Why attack Oceanway?

Before Jagger released her, he leaned in and pressed his lips to hers in a quick kiss. "We'll finish this later."

Oh, yes. They would definitely finish it. But for now, she needed more info on what Zach had said. The Oceanway Coven was run by a Divinity Elder. Eleese Sanders had stepped up the month before to aide in the search for Kalissa when her psycho demon ex-boyfriend had kidnapped her.

Khloe grabbed a pair of jeans and a black T-shirt from the closet and quietly dressed before entering the living room.

Zach had his phone pressed to his ear with the occasional muttered "mmm-hmm," and a final "I'm on it" before he hung up and faced her. "There are three dead and a dozen or so injured. Luckily, they have a Divinity healer and a doctor living in the coven. Bethany is on her way there now to help out."

After she'd laced her Nikes, Khloe stood and walked toward the door. Jagger stepped in front of her. "Where are you going?"

Hands on her hips, she cast him a narrowed-eye gaze. "Move."

"You're not leaving."

"And you're not stopping me."

He stepped closer, trying to crowd her. Or was he trying to intimidate her?

Whatever.

She could teleport to the coven if she had to, but this was way more fun. A smirk lifted the corner of her mouth. She raised an index finger and ran it down the center of his chest to the top of his jeans. She hooked her finger in the waistband and tugged. "You're welcome to come with..." she whispered, her lips inches from his. "And watch my back."

The red in his eyes flared for a second. She stepped around him and headed toward the elevator where Zach stood waiting. She didn't get far before Jagger's large hand wrapped around her bicep, halting her advances.

"You like playing with fire?"

"Yes. It is my favorite element." She extracted her arm from his grip and stepped inside the elevator.

The demon hadn't said a word on the elevator ride and didn't appear very happy as he sat in the backseat of Zach's Camaro. He fisted his hands, and he hadn't taken his eyes off her since leaving the condo. That was fine by her. She wouldn't stay behind. She was a Divinity—born to fight in this war between witches and demons.

"So why was the coven attacked?" she asked over Zach's siren.

"There were four Dark Divine kidnapped."

"Fuck! Did you know they were there?" She glared at him. When he remained silent, she tsked. "And you didn't share this information? Good gods, Zach. There is plenty of room in the Maxville Coven and the Divinity House for them. At least we could have offered to strengthen the coven's wards for better security. I know Eleese was aware that Khan was tracking down all the Dark Divine."

He sighed and shook his head, but he didn't take his eyes from the road. "That's what I told Eleese, but she said they been through too much already and assured me that the children were well hidden."

As his words sank in, alarm rose in her chest. "How old are they?"

He white-knuckled the steering wheel, and a tick formed in his temple. "The two girls are seventeen and fourteen. The boys are eight and three."

"Fuck!" Khloe said again. A low, furious growl from the backseat matched her mood at that moment.

CHAPTER NINE

*J*agger's blood boiled at the scene in front of him. Homes half burned to the ground. Children sobbing, scared witless. Memories of his own village being mowed down by Khan's army flashed in his mind. The terror in his mate's eyes as she drew her last breath, and the pain that gripped his heart as his two-year-old daughter died in his arms. He hadn't been there to protect them, just like no one had been at the coven to guard the witches.

Hands fisted by his sides, he tried to calm himself. He had a mission, and she was more than a handful. The Oracle's words swirled in his mind. The thought that she might have seen Khloe's death fueled the rage Jagger felt toward Khan even more. Because losing another mate would kill him. If not literally, then he would go rogue, and Hecate would have to put him down like a rabid hellhound.

Glancing to his temptress, he noticed Khloe dart off across the small community. A double take had him rushing after her. The twins were supposed to stay separate. What the hell was Kalissa doing here?

With quick strides, he made his way to the twins, who were locked in a tight hug. The rush of panic subsided as he observed the females. Frozen in place, he watched as magic swirled around them in iridescent waves.

"Ayden Daniels." Kalissa's mate stood in front of him with his hand extended.

Jagger gave a short nod and accepted the other male's hand. "Jagger. I guess there's no way to keep them apart."

Ayden chuckled and sent his woman a hungry gaze before speaking. "No. They're a package deal."

What the hell was that supposed to mean? Khloe was his to claim. His body coiled with possessiveness, and he had to stop himself from carting her far away from everyone until she agreed to be his mate.

Ayden flicked his gaze back to Jagger, brow raised as if the man had read his mind. Then with a shake of his head and a smile lifting the corners of his mouth, he explained. "I meant that they can't be separated. Lo is my sister now, and my bond with Kalissa ties us together, too. It was pretty weird at first."

Ah, that made sense. Magical twins had an unbreakable link. They were a part of each other. Through Kalissa and Ayden's mating bond, Khloe was also tied to the couple. And her future husband would complete a quad circle of power.

This newfound acknowledgement raised alarm in him. The trio was a powerful force, one the demons wanted. Were they trying to snag one to lure in the other two? Possible.

He wanted to take Khloe's arm and drag her back to her condo until he could figure out their next step. The urge dissolved when Zach came over with a young strawberry-blond Divinity. Both wore sad expressions.

"The magical residue is too mixed. Eleese can't get a clear reading. There is a demonic essence, but that could be the Dark Divine," Zach announced when he stopped before the group.

Lex flashed in beside Jagger and agreed with the deputy. "I couldn't pick up on any particular trail. They purposely blended scents."

"Do you think there were dark ones with the demons who took them?" Khloe asked as she stepped away from her twin.

"It would be the only way any of this makes sense," Jagger stated flatly. When all eyes shifted his way, he continued his thought. "The wards were strong. I felt the energy when I crossed the perimeter. However, they weren't set to keep the dark ones out."

"Because they had Dark Divine living in the coven." Khloe cursed and began to pace in front of him. "And they could have entered the coven long before the demons did to set them off, catching everyone off guard."

"My mother offers you any and all of her resources. We want them found and brought home safely." It was the young witch who'd approached with Zach who spoke. When everyone turned to her, she shifted shyly. "I'm Desiree. Eleese is my mother."

Jagger felt his brother stiffen beside him. The ever-so-cool, hardened-souled Alexander had actually shown emotion.

In public.

Very interesting.

"We have to find out where they've taken the children," Khloe blurted out.

Her worry turned to determination, and he could see the wheels turning in her head. He didn't like it. Not one bit. The urge to gather her up and carry her back to her condo was almost too strong to resist. But, if he did that, she'd leave on her own. She was too headstrong and proud. No, he had to gain her trust and figure this shit out, then maybe she'd agree to be his mate.

Khloe looked around the room of the home where she'd grown up, now called The Divinity House. Lydia sat in the oversized armchair with the footrest up, cradling a cup of tea between her hands. Her long, red curls were pulled back in a ponytail. She wore a pale green babydoll top and a pair of maternity capri pants.

Melaina Harris, Divinity Elder, sat on the love seat next to Lydia's chair. Her straight black hair and the reddish-brown undertones in her skin gave away her Native American heritage. Khloe didn't know which tribe Mel's ancestors came from. The Elder seemed to be a private person, and Khloe wasn't the type to pry into others' business. She figured Mel would open up when she was ready.

Ayden sat with his arms around Kalissa on the sofa Mel sat on. Khloe loved her new brother-in-law. He was so good for Kalissa, and he'd helped her overcome her dark past and learn to trust her Divine gifts of visions again.

Zach sat at the computer desk, going over surveillance files while watching the two Death

Demons that stood in opposite corners of the living room.

Worry plagued Khloe's mind and tightened her chest at the thought of four helpless, innocent children held against their will. "I want to know how those animals found out they were there," she fumed, coming to a stop as a large body appeared in front of her.

It was much too tempting to place her palms against that sculpted chest and draw from his strength, but it would show a weakness she couldn't afford. She was too vulnerable, and her emotions were too high to deal with the demon. If she touched him right now...

Yeah. Not happening.

Pivoting on her heel, she moved away from Jagger, putting as much distance between them as she could and yet still be in the same room. The Death Demon did things to her that she would have no problem exploring if he were *magickin* or human. That thought brought a frown to her face. Why did it matter if he was a demon?

Yeah, he was arrogant, controlling, and a little over-bearing, but he wasn't evil. Not like other demons. In fact, he seemed to be right on board with helping them in this fight, especially after the destruction of the Oceanway Coven, and the kidnapping of the Dark Divine children. But was he here on his own or just doing his job?

A mental nudge from her twin brought Khloe's eyes to the happy newlyweds. Kalissa didn't trust the Death

Demon. Khloe didn't need the psychic bond with her twin to tell her how Kalissa felt. No, it was the dagger-like stares she sent Jagger. Khloe tamped down her irritation. Her sister had a right to mistrust demons. After all, her ex-boyfriend was half demon and had put her under a spell to steal her from Ayden over fifteen years ago.

"How did they know the Dark Divine were at the coven?" Khloe repeated the question to no one in particular, returning her thoughts to the issue at hand. She had to find those children. "We need to get inside that warehouse."

The warehouse, aka Grayson Distributions, was the mother ship of Demetrius's demonic operations. Khloe had had the chance to peek at the construction plans of the building, and found that the garage under the structure had not been included. She wanted to know why. The only reason she could think of was that they were hiding something down there. She wanted inside.

"I'm working on it." Zach's gruff voice came from the small desk in the corner of the living room. "The damn security on the place is tight."

"I may be able to get in," Khloe announced. There wasn't a technical device made she couldn't breach. At least, she hadn't run across one yet.

"No," a refrain of voices said simultaneously.

She turned to the closest voice. Jagger loomed over her, a wall of hardened muscle. Her lips pressed together in a thin line, and irritation intensified inside her. With her index finger, she poked him in the chest and said, "You don't get to tell me no."

He gripped her hand in his larger one and removed it from his personal space. When he didn't let go, she called the element of Fire. Heat rose and flowed to her hand and into his. He absorbed it and pushed it back to her. Surprised, she sucked in a breath, but not because it was painful. It felt good and awakened every nerve ending in her body. She was shocked that he'd just recharged her fourth element, and they hadn't had sex.

She stared into his chocolate-brown eyes, and then the room around her dissolved. Jagger's magic enveloped her and pulled her through time and space before they materialized inside her condo.

"Seriously?"

Jagger smirked at the fury building inside Khloe as she stared him down with arms crossed. "You're not taking unnecessary risks."

"Just because you were sent here as my guardian doesn't give you the right to control me." She started to pace the living room of her condo. "Besides, I'll take whatever risks are needed to bring back those kids."

"And we'll work together. I can't allow you to sacrifice yourself for information."

Her head snapped up, and she met his gaze. "Were you in my head?" That angered her further. The increased beats of her heart and the intensity of her scent told him that.

"I don't need to be in your head to know what you had planned," he countered.

Narrowing her eyes, she held his stare for several seconds before her phone rang. She answered it without checking who it was. "Yeah."

"Where the hell are you?" Jagger's supernatural hearing picked up Kalissa's scolding tone from the other end of the line.

Khloe let out a huff. "I'm at my condo. Death has decided I need saving from myself."

"I don't like it. There's too much sexual tension between you two. It's distracting."

Jagger froze at Kalissa's observation. A part of him wanted to rejoice at that. If Kalissa felt the tension, then Khloe was experiencing it.

"Yeah, well, try being around you and Ayden all the damn time," Khloe shot back, not denying what her sister said. "I'll deal with Jagger, and we'll meet up in the morning. Call me if you come up with a plan before then."

She hung up the phone and turned toward her bedroom.

"Where are you going?"

"To bed. Make yourself comfortable, in the spare bedroom, over there." She pointed to the room on the opposite side of the condo from hers. Then she walked into her room and slammed the door.

CHAPTER TEN

Khloe landed with the grace of a cat. She climbed down the side of the building, one balcony at a time, until the second story, where she jumped to the ground. She could have teleported, but she didn't want to alert Jagger. She wasn't going to take the chance that the demon would be waiting for her to use magic to leave the condo.

Descending the high-rise was more fun anyway. It gave her muscles a much-needed workout.

She needed space. Time alone, away from her demon guardian. The large, hard-bodied, sexy-as-hell, naturally tanned, luscious Death Demon that made her fantasize about things she'd only read about.

And it was stifling to be around him. He made her want things she hadn't wanted since Mark. Things she couldn't allow herself to have. No way was she going to give her heart to another only to have it squashed.

Demonic energy crawled up her spine, and she shivered. *Damn*. Couldn't a girl get some air?

Khloe retreated into a nearby alley and hid in the shadows. Closing her eyes, she slowed her breathing and drifted into a meditative state. She opened her eyes and waited.

A moment later, two demons passed in front of the alley's opening. One stopped and smelled the air. *Shit*. Demons and their damn sense of smell. She remained pressed against the brick wall of the skyscraper and willed the fuckers to come closer.

Just a little closer. Come to Mama.

A smirk tugged at her lips when the creatures stepped into the alley, confusion etched on their inhuman faces. Khloe and her Divine brethren were the only ones who could see the demons for what they truly were—vile monsters of the Underworld. These two were no exception.

They might have their horns hidden, but the illusion spell that hid their true appearance didn't work on her. She never understood why she could see through illusions and glamours. It was like a sixth sense. While Kalissa could distinguish the differences between a human and a demon, Khloe could see past whatever magic they used to blend into the human world.

Her father had once told her it was because she was special and a very powerful little witch. She had been five when she'd first seen someone perform an illusion spell at the coven. Noah had changed the color of his hair to pure white in a spell-casting class demonstration. However, Khloe saw through the spell after a few seconds. She argued that it hadn't lasted. The other children laughed at her, calling her a freak.

The memory of her father drawing her tear-filled face in his hands and speaking the words that made everything better filled her thoughts. *"You're my special, powerful little witch, and possess the gift of magical sight."*

Her chest tightened, and a lump rose in her throat.

"Love you, Daddy," she whispered into the wind and pushed away from the wall to step out into the middle of the alley.

Stupid and Confused stilled and stared at her like a pair of deer caught in headlights. Their strength was that of a *Lackey*, the lesser of the demon race. Most likely, they were scouts sent out to search. But she could care less what they searched for.

"Hello, boys," she said sweetly.

The one on the right narrowed his eyes on her. "Looks like we have a lost witch. Don't you know it's not safe to wander around here alone? Things could happen to a pretty creature like you."

Her eyebrows rose, and she smiled. "Really? What kinds of things?"

"Oh, terrible things. Too awful to mention." It was the other demon who spoke this time, drawing Khloe's gaze to him. His eyes held lust and greed. It didn't take a genius, or a telepath, to figure out what was going on inside his head.

Ew.

"Come with us. We'll show you the sights. Maybe have a little party afterward." Both demons nodded in unison like toddlers waiting for their favorite cookie to come out of the oven.

Khloe shrugged in a nonchalant way. "As fun as that sounds, I am afraid I'll have to pass."

The males' faces fell into lines of fury. Demons hated to be dismissed. Good.

She stepped back farther into the darkness of the alley. As expected, the demons followed. There was no reason to alert any nosy humans. Another step back, and she hit something solid and froze. She didn't need to turn around to know that two more demons stood behind her.

"Fuck me," she breathed out.

One of the creatures laughed out load. "That offer has already been made. Now you must die."

Jagger lay on the guest bed, staring at the ceiling.

The condo was too quiet, and his nerves made it impossible to sleep.

He rose from the bed and stalked quietly through the living room to Khloe's closed bedroom door. With an ear pressed against the wood, he listened. He frowned and fisted his hands at his sides. She'd left.

How in the hell had she gotten past him? Why hadn't he sensed that she was gone?

Damn it!

Opening one of the floor-to-ceiling glass windows, he shifted into his ghostly shadow and flew out into the night. Fury and fear pushed him to find her. It wasn't that Khloe couldn't take care of herself; it was the manner in which she went about it. In his observation of her in the last month, she had proven her reckless nature and need for an adrenaline rush time and time again.

Jagger was beginning to understand the slight smirk on his mother's beautiful face when she'd appointed him Khloe's guardian. It was just like Hecate to give him a challenge like this.

He slowed and drifted to the ground near an alley holding Khloe's magical signature. Sounds of a struggle followed by a feminine laugh he knew all too well cut through the air. She was in there, and not alone. Still in his shadow form, he eased into the alley.

His angelic Divinity stood holding a dagger in one hand, feet spread in a defensive stance and chest rising in short, even breaths. She had a smile on her face, like she was merely sparring with her sister.

A demon, most likely a Soulkeeper by the yellowish skin tone and markings on his wrists, lay on his back, dead. Three other minor demons—he couldn't pick up on their origin—formed a semicircle in front of Khloe. The demons weren't having as much fun as his mate.

Mate.

Until now, he'd denied it. He couldn't let himself get involved. It was against the rules. He was her guardian, never to be involved more than keeping her safe. But seeing her now was all he could take. She was beautiful beyond any creature he'd ever seen in his three-thousand-plus years of life.

He inched closer, and Khloe's head jerked in his direction. She narrowed her eyes and pursed her lips. Annoyance drifted from her. The other demons sensed him too and took that moment to react. They rushed forward. Jagger returned to solid form, grabbed the closest demon by the neck, and snapped it with a quick twist.

A scream made his heart seize. Khloe was on her knees, holding her side with one hand while gaining her balance to stand with the other. The distraction and fear for his mate cost him. One of the two remaining demons charged at him, knocking him to the ground, farther away from her.

He had to believe she would be okay on her own. She was strong.

A flash of silver from a blade caught his attention, and he rolled just in time for it to miss his heart. Fucking demons were out for blood. Did they not know Khan wanted Khloe alive?

Or, had the game plan changed?

CHAPTER ELEVEN

Khloe pushed away the burning pain in her side. The damn blade had iron in it. Had to. Because now, her side was on fire.

Ah, Fire. She smirked at the demon and raised the element she loved so well. Heat started in her chest and built until she pushed it out to her arms and then her hands. Two fireballs formed in her palms as she lifted them between her and the bastard facing her.

The demon laughed. Pissed at his amusement, she thrust one of the fireballs at him. The fiery sphere hit him square in the chest, but nothing happened. Angry, she flung the other one at him. He absorbed it.

What the hell? She formed a cloud and soaked him with falling rain. Again, the demonic creature absorbed it.

"You can't fight him with the elements," Jagger growled several feet from her.

"Why not?"

"He's a Dark Divine, and appears to be elemental."

A sinking feeling went through her. This demon had waited for his chance, held back while the others met their fate. "He's demonic."

"That why they are called Dark Divine."

She knew that. The irritating Death Demon thought he knew it all, and the lack of focus on her end pissed her off. "So, how do I kill it?" She ducked as her dark counterpart swung at her.

"They can be killed in the same way you can."

That was so not helpful. She had to take his head or take his powers. Khloe chose his head since she didn't know how to drain his powers.

An awful howl startled her. She turned in time to see the demon Jagger fought puff in a cloud of black dust. Her guardian locked gazes with her for a brief second before he lunged for her. She didn't know how, but she heard Jagger tell her to duck. It was like he was inside her mind, but Death Demons weren't telepaths. Not that she knew of anyway.

She moved just in time for Jagger to collide with the Dark Divine. They rolled on the asphalt until Jagger straddled the dark one. A flash of light came from a pendant around Jagger's neck she hadn't noticed before.

The Dark Divine stilled and dissolved away into nothing.

"How did you do that? What did you do?" she asked

with arms crossed. He rose and advanced toward her. The pendant glowed with a brilliant ice-blue light. At closer inspection, the charm looked identical to the Sinew. "Hey! That's supposed to be with Teddy-Bear."

"The Sinew is with the hounds. This is just a piece of it. You don't think Hecate let all the world's magic out of her control, do you?" He grinned at her. She swallowed, not liking how that smile affected her. She looked away when he came to a stop inches from her.

"Why did you go out on your own?"

She raised her eyes to his icy glare. "I'm a big girl. Besides, I was doing fine until you showed up like a dark knight come to save the day."

One dark brow rose, and the corner of his mouth lifted slightly. "Dark knight?"

She rolled her eyes. "You sure aren't a white knight, demon." She turned from him and walked out of the alley, her side still burning like hell.

A groan escaped her as Jagger fell into step beside her. He held out a hand. "Come back to the condo so we can take care of your wound. It won't heal until it's cleaned."

Like she needed him to tell her that. The dagger the demon had used had iron particles on it, which would cling to her skin. If she didn't get the cut cleaned out soon, the iron could enter her bloodstream and possibly kill her. "I don't need a teleporting escort."

He made a sound close to a growl before speaking. "Why do you resist my assistance?"

She stopped walking and faced him. "Because I don't like you."

Khloe faded out, her body disappearing in a soft white glow. Jagger shook his head. She was going to be the death of him. That fiery temper of hers would send him over the edge. He had a hard enough time controlling his lusty urges around her. That control would snap very soon.

With one last look around, he teleported back to the condo. He went directly to her bedroom. Light spilled out from her bathroom where she stood in front of the sink in her jeans and a bra, frantically cleaning the open cut on her side. Her scent was filled with panic and fear.

Khloe's teal gaze met his. "It's too late. The iron is in my blood. I feel it." Tears filled her eyes.

In one long stride, he stood nose to nose with her and captured her face in his hands. "I can help, but I need your permission. I can draw the iron out of your blood. Do you understand?"

She shook her head then stilled, eyes growing round. "You have to bite me. No…"

"Lo, please. It's the only way."

Silence overtook her as though she were weighing her options, of which there were none. "What will that do to me?"

"The bite? Nothing besides save your life."

She gasped, wrapped her arms around her stomach, and sank to the floor at his feet. "Do it. Just make it stop burning."

Jagger scooped her up in his arms and carried her to the bed. Carefully, he laid her down and knelt beside the bed. He rested one hand against her creamy skin over her rib cage. She flinched as if not expecting the touch. His fangs elongated, yet he stalled. Uncertainty and guilt rode him hard. Once he took her blood, he'd be linked to her for the rest of her existence. She was his mate. The bite would only confirm it and seal what was fated. There would be no turning back. No re-do button.

"Jagger, for gods' sake, do it!" she demanded through clenched teeth. By the sound of it, she was also fighting a scream.

Her pain reached out to him, and he lost the ability to think. He struck, sinking his fangs into her soft skin around the wound, and sucked. A moan drifted through the air, and he wasn't sure if it was his or Khloe's. Nor did he care.

The rich, tangy, sweet taste of her was intoxicating.

The scent of chocolate with a hint of rose filled him as her blood flowed down his throat to mingle with his.

Under his hands, she began to relax. Her breathing slowed, returning to normal. With his fangs inside her, a connection formed, so strong he could feel her subsiding pain and increasing arousal.

A few more pulls and the iron would be out of her system. He withdrew his fangs and stared down at the wound. The cut was knitting itself together, healing with the Divine magic that ran through her veins, and now his.

Chilled fingers touched his cheek, bringing his eyes to hers. Like a siren's call, she beckoned him closer until their lips touched.

None-too-gently, he thrust his tongue inside her mouth and twined it with hers. She wrapped her arms around his neck, sank her fingers into his hair, and drew him in deeper.

By force of will, he pulled back and broke the kiss. "I need to go."

CHAPTER TWELVE

"*Y*ou can't leave."

He was out of his mind if he thought he would leave her all hot and bothered.

"I have to." Jagger's chest rose and fell in breathless waves. Pools of his emotions washed over her.

"Why?"

He was in her face before she could blink. "Because if I don't leave now, you will regret it in the morning."

Yes, that was more like it. She'd been worried for a minute that she was the only one fighting the lusty urges. Now the truth had come out. "Maybe not," she whispered against his lips.

He cursed.

"Khloe, you don't know what you're asking. You're hyped up on adrenaline, and your magic is running wild in your blood, repairing the damage."

Who was he trying to convince? She lived her life

by taking chances and never looking back. Maybe in a few centuries, she'd feel differently, but she was young, and she would enjoy the ride as long as she could.

She opened her mouth to speak, but he shook his head. "I am beyond control right now with your blood in my veins. I can't promise I'll be gentle."

A smile tugged at her lips, and naughty thoughts circled around inside her head. "Maybe I want to be possessed, controlled."

Broad shoulders bunched and flexed as he shifted to hover over her. Heat coursed through her in anticipation. "You ever fuck a demon?"

"Never thought about it."

Her sex throbbed with a need she'd never known. She was growing tired of being alone, but couldn't give her heart to anyone fully, especially since Mark had ripped it out.

Jagger captured her mouth in a demanding kiss. When his tongue ran across the seam of her lips, she opened and welcomed the invasion. The sweet tang of her blood on his tongue was oddly arousing.

She ran her hand under his shirt and over the hard muscles of his chest and smiled at the light dusting of hair. He pulled back from the kiss, yanked the shirt over his head, and tossed it to the floor.

She chewed on her bottom lip and marveled at the creamed-coffee-colored skin of his body. He grasped her hands when she reached out to touch him and held them above her head with one of his. His clasp was firm, but it didn't hurt. It did, however, keep her from moving her arms. He lowered his body to pin hers in place.

His hard length pressed into her through their jeans. She moaned out a plea. Jagger had reduced her to begging, and she didn't care. Sex with Jagger somehow felt right. Besides, the need got worse the longer they were together. She had to get it out of the way. End the desire to have him once and for all.

When he'd sunk his fangs into her moments ago, she'd lost all hope of controlling her urges. That was the moment she knew she had to have him. Feel his power surge through her with every pounding thrust.

A low growl brought her eyes up to meet his, now completely red and glowing with need. "You said you couldn't read my mind," she teased.

"I can't. I can smell your desire." He leaned down and pressed his lips to the top of her left breast.

She sucked in a gasp and arched into him. Her body warmed from the inside out, starting at the center of her chest and spreading out to her limbs and head until she was consumed by a raging inferno of lust and desire.

Jagger abandoned her breast, and she whimpered in protest. He let go of her hands and moved down her body. His soft lips touched her belly, and she jumped. A low chuckle vibrated off her skin. She giggled at the sensation and then moaned when his tongue drew her belly button ring into his mouth.

"I thought you didn't want to take this slow."

He lifted up on all fours over her. A wicked grin spread across his face. "I've changed my mind. I have found I enjoy torturing you."

For the love of the gods. She was going to die a very happy and pleasured woman.

Warm breath glided over her skin as he trailed light kisses back up her body. With a swipe of his hand, her bra disappeared. She gasped when he took a nipple into his mouth. Hot need shot straight to her core, causing the walls of her sex to pulse.

When his tongue flicked the hardened bud, she fisted the sheet and rubbed her throbbing pussy against his erection. It did nothing to ease the ache. There was too much clothing between them. Unclenching the sheet, she slid one hand between them to unbutton his jeans.

Jagger raised his head and seized her hand in his. Her heart skipped a beat at the fierce desire showing in his gaze. "Are you sure?" His tone was low and graveled.

She had never been sure of anything. Until now. If she didn't get the release her body screamed for, she wouldn't be held responsible for her actions. "Yes."

A fraction of a second later, both of them were completely naked. That wicked grin was back on her demon's face. Living in the human world as a mortal, she didn't use her magic for simple daily tasks, like dressing and undressing. Being with Jagger, she was free to explore all her magical abilities and didn't have to hide from the prejudices of some humans.

"I could've done that."

"But you didn't."

She didn't have time to respond before his mouth was on hers, and his tongue had thrust inside, searching for hers. Her moan changed to a gasp as his cock slid inside her.

He stopped halfway in and broke the kiss. Their eyes locked on one another's. A tic formed in his jaw as if he were trying to fight for control. After a brief silence, he thrust in the rest of the way, filling her. She was lost. Lost in the sensation of being consumed and taken by Jagger.

She wrapped her legs around his waist and moved in sync to his gentle thrusting. With her tongue, she drew his earlobe into her mouth and gently bit down. A growl rumbled from his chest, and he quickened his pace.

Pleasure built from the depths of her being until her climax threw her over the edge, ripping a scream of pleasure from her. Jagger followed her over with his own release.

CHAPTER THIRTEEN

*M*orning sunlight bathed the bedroom with the signs of a new day. Warmth enveloped Khloe, and she smiled. That warmth wasn't from the sun. It was from the large arms wrapped around her, cradling her in a protective shelter.

Reluctantly, Khloe slid out of bed and went to the bathroom. She closed the door with a soft click and turned on the shower. She felt invigorated, alive, complete somehow. What an odd feeling. The last time she'd felt so at peace was...

Oh, no. She wasn't going there. Mark might have been her magical companion—eternal life partner—but he'd taken all hope of a family away from her the day he'd rejected what she was. No one knew if Divinities could have more than one perfect mate in a lifetime.

Khloe was in no hurry to find out.

After taking a quick shower, she opened the bathroom door and was hit with the wonderful aroma of coffee. She followed her nose toward the smell and leaned against the bar-style countertop separating the kitchen from the living room. Jagger was making breakfast. Bacon sizzled on the stove while he chopped veggies. The carton of eggs and a small pile of shredded cheese told her he was making omelets.

"You can cook?" She couldn't keep the giggle from escaping.

Jagger lifted his head to face her. She stifled a gasp. Her heart rate skipped five beats at the raw energy coming from him. It reached out to her and caressed her skin like a physical touch. Thoughts of the night before flashed in her mind and stirred all kinds of unwanted need.

He set down the knife and stalked toward her like a predator after his prey. One large arm snaked around her waist and drew her into his body. Her breasts flattened against his chest while his lips possessed hers in a fiery kiss. His tongue invaded her mouth, but she didn't fight it, didn't want to.

Her heart raced as their lips moved together and tongues tangled in an erotic dance. Jagger sent her places no other man had dared. It might be because he was a demon, or because of his connection to the Sinew, but whatever it was, she liked it. Liked the way he smelled, tasted and felt under her, on top of her, and inside her. He was fast becoming her new addiction. Far more so than Mark...

With a hand flat against Jagger's chest, Khloe pushed, breaking the kiss. His inquisitive eyes met hers. Breathlessly, she managed to say, "The bacon's burning."

His sensual lips lifted in a smirk, and he gave her a quick kiss before releasing her and stepping back to tend to the splattering bacon. She turned and walked to the wall of windows in her living room. The beautiful view of the river and cityscape was peaceful on the weekend mornings.

She opened the double doors and stepped out onto her balcony. Fresh air mixed with the scent of salt water and the aroma of coffee from the factory across the river greeted her. With a deep breath, she drew in the air and connected to the elements around her. Realization was starting to settle in. Her reaction to Jagger was all too familiar, and she cursed herself for not picking up on it sooner. Like before, she'd spent the best night of her life with him.

Damn it. Lo, when you step in it...

This wasn't happening, couldn't happen. No. Her imagination was running rampant. Worry for the Dark Divine children had raised her stress levels and pushed her senses into overdrive. That had to be it, and not the fact that Jagger could be her magical mate.

A steamy cup of coffee appeared in front of her face. She flinched involuntarily but took the cup. She followed Jagger with her gaze as he leaned against the railing and studied her.

"You're tense. Why?"

She took a sip of coffee and moved her gaze to the river below. "I'm worried about the children."

He reached out to caress her cheek, and she stepped back. His eyebrows dipped in a frown before he said, "Let's eat breakfast and then go to the Divinity House to check in with your sister."

Khloe moved toward the door, stopped, and turned to face him. "For the record, I still don't like you."

As soon as she entered her family's farmhouse, Khloe darted off to the downstairs master suite in search of her sister, leaving Jagger alone in the living room. She had to focus on finding the children and not dwell on the fantasy of finding a second mate, especially with a hot-as-hell, passionate Death Demon.

That's what you get for being so impulsive.

Her impulsive nature was what got her heart broken the first time. She'd jumped at the thought of having a mate to share her long life with and had spilled all her secrets without a thought to how he would react. She should have known better, but her instincts weren't one of her strengths. Her ability to think and react quickly, however, had gotten her out some sticky situations. She laughed, thinking of the times when her jump-in-and-go-for-it personality had gotten her into trouble just as much.

Opening the bedroom door, she was greeted by an eerie silence along with an odd feeling.

"Close the door." Kalissa's soft voice drifted from the bathroom.

With her heart sinking to her stomach, Khloe did as she was asked and slowly walked to the bathroom. Inside, Kalissa sat on the edge of the tub, staring at something in her hands, a mixture of shock, happiness, and fear coloring her face. Chest tightening at the possibility that something terrible had happened, Khloe advanced closer. Her twin lifted her gaze, then Khloe saw what was in Lis's hand.

A pregnancy test.

All fear fell away as though washed out by a tidal wave. Khloe dropped to her knees in front of her sister and took the test. Two pink lines. She squeaked and grabbed Kalissa in a tight hug.

"I'm scared, Lo."

Drawing back to meet her stare, Khloe smiled. "You set the psycho on fire. Nothing scares you anymore."

Kalissa laughed and took the stick back to study it. "We're in the middle of a war. What if I'm not a good mother?"

"Don't be silly. You'll be perfect. If anyone was born to raise dozens of happy babies, it was you." She took her sister by the hands and stood. "And Ayden will be a great father. Does he know?"

"He told me to take the test."

"Damn empath." Khloe tugged her laughing sister toward the living room.

After breakfast, Khloe snapped back into her stay-the-hell-out-of-my-way mood. Jagger liked her playful, sensual side from the night before better. This new side of her was different from when they'd first met. She was closed off, as though she didn't trust him, or herself. They didn't speak when they'd first arrived at Divinity House. Instead, she'd pushed past him to find her sister. All he could do was watch her rear end move as she walked away.

"She's a handful."

Jagger jerked his head towards the voice now entering the house behind him. Zach. The empath needed an off button. "It's rude to read people's emotions without permission."

A familiar presence came into the room from the kitchen. "You don't need to be an empath to know what you are thinking or feeling, brother."

"Can it, Lex."

A knowing gleam appeared in Lex's eyes but vanished when the twins came into the room, and the very pregnant Lydia stepped off the bottom step of the staircase.

Kalissa and Lydia took a seat on the sofa while Khloe picked up a remote control. A white screen lowered from the ceiling, and she fired up a laptop. Zach moved in to set up a projector.

Jagger was confused about what they were doing until the screen filled with the same image as the computer. "A map?"

"That's not just any map. It's the blueprints for the warehouse that is currently Grayson Distributions." Khloe's voice held a hint of mischief. He stared at her, unsure where she was going with this display. She rolled her eyes. "I hacked into the security system. I also have live video."

"When?" Jagger hadn't noticed her slip away.

"It's what I was working on at breakfast."

"Unfortunately, it tells us nothing," Zach said in disgust.

"That's why I think we should go down there. Snoop around a little."

Zach shook his head at Khloe. "That's breaking and entering."

"That's bullshit, Zachary! These are demons. Human laws don't apply to them." Her distress laced her voice, and her teal eyes flashed darker.

Jagger moved closer to Khloe as Zach's magical signature darkened slightly. It wasn't enough to alert anyone but him, and maybe Lex, but he still didn't like the feeling there was something under the deputy's easy-going front.

"I'm going in," Khloe announced.

"Not alone," the group said at once.

The twins locked gazes, and Jagger guessed they were telepathically conversing. After a few seconds, Kalissa threw up her hands and left the room.

"I won't be alone," Khloe spoke loud enough so that her voice carried throughout the lower floor. "Jagger's going with me."

CHAPTER FOURTEEN

The sun was setting by the time Khloe and Jagger materialized a couple of blocks from the warehouse where Demetrius—Khan's demon general—played human businessman and owner of Grayson Distributions, a medical supply company.

Zach had given orders to wait for him and Ayden before making a move. Apparently, the demons brought out the serious side of his cop. That irritated the hell out of Khloe. She was more than capable of taking care of herself.

Kalissa normally would have accompanied her husband on a mission like this, especially since the two of them were more powerful as a bonded pair. But not today, or anytime in the next eight months or so. Khloe smiled. She was going to be an aunt. Oh, how she planned to spoil the hell out of the little one.

"They're here." Jagger's voice brought her out of her

pleasant musings. She shifted her gaze to the next block over.

"Okay, so why can't we mind link? Ayden and I can, and I know you can with any one of us."

Jagger narrowed his eyes like she should know the answer but explained anyway. "Demons will pick up on the magical energy it takes to link together."

And electronic gadgets were out. They couldn't take the chance the demons had something to detect radios and other communication devices. Much to her displeasure, the men thought it was a better plan to go in quiet and undetected.

Completely against her nature.

Patience was not her strongest attribute. In fact, she didn't remember a time when she was successful at waiting for anything, and waiting outside a building crawling with demons was so not what she wanted to do. Nope. She wanted to charge in and take as many of those fuckers out as she could.

She needed a distraction before impulse took her over. "What are they doing?" she growled in irritation.

"I'll flash over and see what they want to do." She jerked her head in his direction, eyebrow raised. He chuckled and leaned into her to whisper in her ear. "I'm a demon. They won't be looking for my energy."

His scent was too tantalizing, too seductive. She had to turn her head away. She didn't want him to know how much his warm breath on her neck affected her. If she peered into his dark brown eyes any longer, she'd have a distraction neither of them needed.

She felt Jagger's presence fade, and she turned to watch him materialize behind Zach and Ayden. Zach jumped, and Khloe stifled a giggle. She was betting Jagger's mouth twitched.

A slight burning sensation on the inside of her left forearm startled her. She turned her arm over and cursed. Her fear was confirmed at the sight of the faded second rose, mirroring the one she'd been born with. *Fuck.* She should be happy to get a second chance, a second life companion. Her perfect mate...was a demon.

But could she trust that this one wouldn't feed her to the wolves?

Jagger popped in beside her. She glared at him, waiting for an answer. "They said to wait and watch the loading area."

"Great. That's exciting."

The heat of his body enveloped her, and she stilled. His lips brushed her ear as he spoke. "I can think of a few things to pass the time."

So could she...Wait. Damn. He thought to lure her in with his seductive whispers? And his incredible body?

She spun around to face him and instantly regretted it. The red swirls in his chocolate-brown eyes glowed with passion. Her body heated with her rising desire as memories of their tangled, naked bodies took over her thoughts.

"Stop." She managed a firm, calm voice and placed her palm on his chest.

Jagger encircled her wrist with his strong fingers and brought her hand to his mouth. Desire raced through her like a raging river. His lips moved to her wrist, and he froze.

He held out her arm where the two of them could see her Divine Roses. "When did this show?"

She closed her eyes and took a deep breath. His voice held more amusement than anger. He probably guessed the answer but needed her to confirm it, and he would make her say it. Damn him. "Just now. And it's not yours."

Maybe if she convinced herself, it would go away. Her heart wouldn't survive another betrayal from another supposed mate.

The look in Jagger's eyes told her he was about to call her bluff. All of a sudden, he stopped and tilted his head to the side as if listening to something. Khloe started to ask what it was, but he placed a finger over her lips to silence her. If there had been no danger of demons finding them, she would have taken that finger into her mouth and teased him with her tongue.

His eyes flicked to meet hers. He leaned into her and brushed his lips against hers. "Save those naughty thoughts for later."

"Are you reading my mind?"

"Nope, just smelling your desire." He said it in that low, seductive whisper he used to melt her. Damn demon senses. He probably knew that her attempts to push him away were failing.

"Two *Lackeys* pulled up to the loading dock."

"What are we waiting for? Let's grab the bastards for questioning."

"We'll do this together."

"Okay, you grab one, and I'll get the other. Then we can take turns pounding them until they sing." A half-smile lifted the right side of his mouth. She returned it with one of her own. "You like that idea."

"Together, Khloe." He leaned into her, crushing her back against the wall, and captured her lips in a dominating kiss.

He released her, and she staggered to the edge of the corner to peer at the two demons as they unloaded the truck. These two didn't even try to hide what they were. Their true demon forms shone like neon lights over a nightclub. One had blue and gray marbled skin and long, silver hair. The other had a red tint to his skin and short, black hair.

Demons were classified by their strengths and abilities. The skin color almost never mattered. Jagger and his brother were called Death Demons because their powers were one step below that of the gods. At one time, they'd served the Underworld gods by collecting the souls of the dead to bring over into the Afterworld.

The *Lackeys* a few yards away from Khloe were

considered nobodies, servants of the *Regals* and *Amiddians*—the upper and middle classes of demons, according to power and influence.

"What are we waiting on?" Khloe clenched her teeth. She hated to wait. Gods knew those vile creatures hadn't waited to kill her parents or snatch those innocent children. Jagger remained silent beside her. Her patience was starting to run super thin, and her muscles twitched. She couldn't stand it any longer and darted around the corner. Jagger's curse followed her as she crept along the wall closest to the delivery truck.

He came up beside her and growled, "Together."

"Hush," she snapped and watched the demons carry boxes from the back of the truck to inside the warehouse. They were close enough to be heard by the *Lackeys*.

From her position, she could still see Zach and Ayden. Both of them looked less than pleased with her. Oh, well. They'd get over it. She was going to find out where those kids were.

She turned toward Jagger and gasped at how close he was. With a palm flat on his chest, she whispered, "Go to the other side and we'll block them in. I'm hoping Zach and Ayden figure out what we are doing." She started to turn back to the *Lackeys* but remembered something. "You can tell them, right?"

"Wait. Here."

His two clipped words were heavy with annoyance and sounded too much like a demand. She'd have to deal with his bossy ass later. That thought brought a frown to her face. She had to get away from him and clear her head. Jagger was slipping further into her life the more time they spent together.

She knew the minute he materialized behind her, but she remained still and refused to give him even a fraction of her attention. He stepped into her and pressed his front to her back. With his lips inches from her neck, he whispered, "They're going to come from the other side of the building. We move in together."

She shivered as his warm breath caressed her sensitive skin and slightly cursed her weakness. With a nod, she stepped away from him.

A few seconds later, Ayden and Zach appeared at the opposite corner of the building. The demons were trapped. Zach counted on his fingers to give the go-ahead. Once his third finger went up, they moved in as a team.

The demons saw Zach and Ayden first and tried to run, only to come to a halt a few feet from Khloe and Jagger. She smiled and stalked toward them. Jagger muttered a protest, which she ignored. He would learn she wasn't easily controlled. Well, at least outside the bedroom.

Trapped like a couple of bunnies facing a pack of wolves, the demons looked confused but determined. They searched the area with their gazes. Then they stilled and listened.

Khloe backed up into Jagger. "What's coming?"

Whatever it was, it could only be heard by supernatural hearing. Most humans might classify the Divinities as supernatural, but they were more like humans than most wanted to admit. Meaning no ultra sensitive hearing or night vision.

"Others are coming."

"How many?"

"Not sure. A couple. Maybe more."

The words hadn't completely left Jagger's lips before the metal door slammed opened and out came three large *Amiddians*.

The *Lackeys* took the distraction as an opportunity to strike. The blue-skinned demon came at Khloe. She braced for impact as he barreled into her, knocking her to her back. Pain rode every nerve ending, and she bit back a scream. A wave of magic washed over her, familiar and pure. It was Ayden. Of that, she was sure.

Drawing in a deep breath and soaking up the magic through her pores, she concentrated on healing. She willed herself to move. A second later, she was able to buck the demon off her and send him flying over her head.

She stood and conjured a dagger. A scream made her whip her head around in time to see the reddish-skinned demon dissolve into ash with a smirking Jagger standing over it. Damn, her demon was sexy.

His muscles contracted as his chest rose and fell with deep, even breaths. As though sensing her, he turned and came at her and didn't stop until they were nose-to-nose. He closed the few inches of space between them and snaked one of his large arms around her waist. Before she could protest, his lips pressed against hers.

He broke the kiss and thrust his hand out to the side. Blinking rapidly to clear the fog from her mind, she looked to see another pile of demon ash at their feet. "Damn," she breathed out.

Ayden and Zach were holding their own with one demon each. She scanned the area. "Hey, Jag. Wasn't there another *Amiddian*?"

A high-pitched alarm sounded within the building. Jagger met her eyes. "Reinforcements," he said as he grabbed Khloe by the upper arm and dragged her away from the building with his super-human speed. Just before flashing from the scene, he called over his shoulder, "Abort!"

CHAPTER FIFTEEN

"*Y*ou really need to stop teleporting me around like a child." Khloe shoved at Jagger the moment they took form inside Divinity House and walked off.

If they'd been alone, he'd silence that sharp tongue of hers by putting it to good use. But they weren't alone, and the situation with the demons had just gotten more complex.

"They knew we were there," Zach blurted out as he flashed inside the living room and sat down on the sofa.

"It might be a coincidence that they were there." Ayden pulled his wife into a hug and kissed the top of her head as soon as he sat beside her.

Teddy-Bear raised their large heads off the floor where they lay in front of the fireplace. "Nothing with demons is a coincidence," Teddy said with a snort.

Bear shook his head. "Nope. They are smarter than they look. Well, some of them are."

"If they didn't know before you got there…" Teddy started.

"…they knew when you arrived," Bear finished.

Khloe came back into the room with a tray and set it on the coffee table. "I think your source is feeding both sides, Zachary." Annoyance was evident in her tone. She picked up a package of crackers and handed them to Kalissa then proceeded to pour tea.

"I don't think so. She's as much a part of this war as the rest of us."

"How so?" Kalissa asked.

The doorbell chimed, halting Zach's reply.

Teddy-Bear rose and followed Ayden to the door.

A few moments later, Ayden returned with Desiree Sanders from the Oceanway Coven.

Khloe stepped closer to the other Divinity with concern etched on her features. "Is everything okay?"

Desiree's ice-blue gaze scanned the others in the living room. She wrung her gloved hands nervously in front of her. "Yes. Everything is fine." She looked at Jagger then peered past him to Lex at the kitchen bar. "I want to join the fight."

Khloe crossed her arms. "Just like that? Have you ever fought a demon?"

"Lo," Kalissa warned.

"She can fight, or at least she can defend herself."

Lex broke his usual silence and stood from the barstool to move closer to Desiree.

Jagger studied the witch again. She was small, very young—maybe in her early twenties—and very powerful. Lex had picked up on something he couldn't. By the way Teddy-Bear stood in front of her, the hellhounds did, as well.

Her shoulders dropped. "My ruling elements are Fire and Spirit. I'm also a *Porter.*"

"Aren't *Porters* dangerous?"

"No, Khloe. Considering they all went extinct about three thousand years ago." It was Zach's turn to be annoyed.

Kalissa stood and offered her hand to Desiree. "Come in and sit. Everyone has apparently taken their rude-ass pills today."

Desiree offered a weak smile. "It's okay. After the attack on my coven, I thought it was time to put my undesirable gifts to use."

Khloe laughed. "In that case, welcome to the war." She extended her own offer to sit, but Desiree shook her head and said she had to get back to the coven to help her mother.

After she'd left, Jagger shifted closer to Khloe when she settled into an armchair. His thoughts were on Desiree and the news of her being a *Porter.* Her power would certainly up the Divinities' game plan. With the right training, she could become even more lethal.

Khloe's pinky finger extended out and brushed against his leg, bringing him out of his musings. At first, he thought it was unintentional, but she didn't remove her hand and continued to caress him with light, circular motions just above his knee. Waves of desire rolled through him until it was almost too much to take. He didn't dare move or respond for fear she'd stop.

When her hand wrapped around the back of his knee, he almost lost control. Quickly, he stepped away from her and walked to the back door. The crisp, winter, night air greeted him as he stepped onto the back porch. He took deep breaths with his eyes closed and tried to calm his mind. That was next to impossible with Khloe invading his every thought.

The scent of chocolate with a hint of rose reached him and stroked like tiny caresses all over his body. "Do you need something?" He didn't dare turn around. She was too much of a temptation.

"I wanted to talk to you." It was a soft-spoken request.

He turned to face her. Teal eyes rimmed in jade holding a mixture of fear, desire, and something else he couldn't quite place stared back at him. "What's wrong?"

"I can't do this again, Jagger." She looked away and leaned against the railing.

"Do what again?"

She shrugged. "This…whatever this is between us can't happen. I won't allow it."

"I don't think you can stop what's fated." Jagger stepped closer to her.

Khloe shook her head. "I can. I do have a choice." She turned around, and with his night vision, he saw the hint of tears threatening to spill between her lids.

He reached out and stroked her cheek with the backs of his fingers. "Who hurt you?" May the gods help whoever it was. She gave another shake of her head and moved to leave. He wrapped his arms around her from behind and pressed his lips to her cheek. "Stop running," he whispered.

She took a deep, shaky breath. "It was five years ago. Mark was human...*is* human. He was my magical partner. The one thing precious to my kind."

He knew all too well about finding the one person fated to share a prolonged life with. He'd gone the last three thousand fifty-two years believing he'd never find his until he saw Khloe. But he remained quiet and let her speak.

"I tried to explain what it meant and that he would take my lifespan through the binding ritual." She paused. Jagger hugged her closer. "He...he said I was a black witch come to take his soul. He even went to the newspaper and sold an article about the coven being full of black witches." Khloe turned in his arms and wrapped hers around his waist. "I've never been so destroyed and hurt in my life. You see... I can't do that again."

Jagger let out a chuckle. When she tried to pull

away, he held her in place. "I'm sorry. I'm not laughing at you. It's just ironic."

"How so?" Her tone held anger and annoyance.

"I'm a soul-stealing demon." He laughed again, unable to stop himself.

Khloe relaxed in his arms, and a few seconds later, her shoulders shook with laughter. She lifted her head and smiled at him. "You don't steal souls. You guide them to the Afterworld."

"To this human, there's no difference. Is he still alive?"

"Yes, with his human wife and a kid on the way."

They were silent for a few moments. Jagger was enjoying holding her, the feel of her body fitting perfectly against his. He lifted her chin with his index finger and softly kissed her.

A moan escaped her as she pressed into him and deepened the kiss. He growled in acceptance of her forwardness. That was his Khloe, taking what she wanted. He was going to give her everything he could.

The familiar presence of his brother made him growl in frustration. He broke the kiss and faced his brother's smirk.

"Hecate wishes to speak to both of us. Now." Lex then turned and walked toward the barn.

"Will you be back?"

Jagger cocked his head, confused by her question. "Of course. Why do you ask?"

She shrugged and waved it off as though it didn't matter. "I don't know."

"I promised you we'd find those children. I never break promises." Besides, he could never leave her side longer than he had to. She was his, and he was going to keep her for as long as he lived.

After a quick kiss, he flashed to the Afterworld to meet with the goddess.

What was she doing? Khloe was falling for the demon. Hard. The more time they spent together, the harder it would be to let him go when the children were recovered, and Demetrius's plans to control the Dark Divine were derailed.

And it was all her internal love meter's fault.

She peered down at her birthmark, now double red roses. One was slightly darker than the other. A smile formed on her lips. Jagger wasn't evil by any means, but he was a demon. It made sense that his rose was a deeper red, almost burgundy.

A moment later, Kalissa walked out onto the porch

and leaned against the railing next to her. Khloe laid her head on her twin's shoulder and sighed. "I'm not sure I can do it."

"You really don't have much of a choice. Of course, you could deny it and go your separate ways, but you'd never be complete." Khloe raised her head and studied her sister's profile. Kalissa spoke from experience. She had been lost during those fifteen years away from Ayden, no thanks to the memory spell her psycho ex had put on her to keep them apart. Khloe had watched her cut off the world and withdraw from family and friends without a clue as to why. Would that happen to her if she chose not to mate with Jagger?

"But when Mark and I broke up, after I got over the pain, I didn't feel incomplete."

Kalissa shrugged. "Maybe Mark wasn't your true partner."

"What do you mean?"

"Of course, you two were in love and compatible up until you told him about us and our world. You could have lived a very long life together, happily. But things happen for a reason. Maybe Mark has a different path to walk. Maybe he's not meant to be a part of this war." Kalissa twisted to face her and frowned. "Why are you crying?"

"Because you're pregnant, and I think I'm getting your hormone imbalance. And you sounded like Mom just now." Her sister laughed, and Khloe couldn't stop herself from returning the laugh.

"It doesn't work that way, and you know it." Kalissa took her hand and tugged her to the door. "Think about what I said. Don't pass up the chance to have your true life partner."

Khloe nodded, not wanting to argue with her sister. She would think about what she'd said. Hell, she agreed with most of what Kalissa had said about Mark. But, could Jagger truly be hers? Did he want to spend the rest of his existence tied to her?

The living room lights were dimmed, and furniture had been moved to the side to reveal the three-foot-diameter circle etched in chalk on the hardwood floor. Four white candles were lit and placed around the circle at each directional point. Melaina stood inside the circle and held a small mirror in her hand.

"What's going on?" Worry filtered through Khloe's mind. Surely her twin wouldn't cast a spell on her. That was just wrong.

Kalissa giggled, obviously reading her thoughts. "No spells, silly. We're calling Barbra. Ayden suggested we ask her to spy on the demons."

"Oh." Embarrassment crept up her cheeks. She was becoming paranoid of everything and everyone around her. Man, she had to get a grip. Then Kalissa's words sank in. "That's a great idea. Do you think she'll do it?"

Barbra Loomis was Liam's—Kalissa's psycho ex-boyfriend—mother. She'd hung herself ten years before, after discovering that her husband was a demon. Apparently, Barbra had *magickin* blood in her family, so she was given a choice of being a spirit guide or spending the rest of eternity with her human ancestors in Heaven. She'd chosen to serve the Divinities as their spirit guide, kind of like their guardian angel.

"I'm certain she will." Kalissa paused for a passionate kiss from her husband that was enough to make Khloe blush, which was a hard thing to do.

With a smile, Khloe walked into the circle and rolled her eyes. Mel cracked a smile.

A few moments later, Kalissa joined them inside the circle. "Where is hubby going?" Khloe asked.

"Shower and then to bed."

"Oh, I guess we need to hurry then." Khloe dodged Kalissa's hand swat.

She wondered if it took the three of them to call a ghost. The question was answered when Kalissa took the mirror from Mel and held it flat between them. Khloe couldn't help but ask, "So, how do you call a ghost?"

Her sister didn't bother to look up at her. "Hush and watch."

Khloe pressed her lips together to keep the laugh from escaping. Kalissa's maternal instincts were kicking in already. Next, she'd get the snap of the fingers. A giggle bubbled up and out of her lips. Kalissa's eyes snapped up and narrowed at her. "Sorry." Taking a deep breath, she focused on the task.

As one, they closed their eyes. Khloe focused on her

twin's voice and let the words take her into the meditation needed to start the chant.

After Kalissa spoke the last word of the chant, the air in the room grew thicker. Khloe opened her eyes in time to see a flash of light so brief she wasn't sure she'd seen it.

Barbra's solid form appeared in a white, floor-length gown. Her dark chestnut hair was beautiful against the dress and her milky skin. Her eyes lifted as she smiled brightly at Kalissa. "Lissa, darling, is everything okay?"

Kalissa opened the circle and returned the smile. "We are well." She went on to tell the ghost about the missing Dark Divine children and asked if she'd help.

Barbra didn't hesitate. "Sure. What's the plan?"

CHAPTER SIXTEEN

*J*agger twitched at leaving Khloe behind, while at the same time, he was relieved to get away to meet with Hecate. Not only did he have to give her a report on the Dark Divine, he also wanted to ask about his biological mother and how to contact her.

After materializing in the living room of the home he and Lex had lived in with Hecate for the last couple of centuries, Jagger sensed the goddess's rage. It was dark and thick in the air. A moment later, she entered the living room. She glared at them as if waiting for them to share something positive.

Jagger frowned and shook his head. He didn't need to tell her they had no good news. So he and Lex remained silent.

"I draw the line when children are in the line of fire. Khan is doing something to block me from seeing him and his demons." She paced, curling and uncurling her hands while her magic spiraled around her. "I need the two of you on the front lines with the Divinities. Khan will not win this."

When she paused, Jagger took that moment to tell her his theory about the Sinew and Khloe. "I believe the demons have a piece of the Sinew, and they are looking for someone strong enough to charge it."

"That I know. They will not succeed because you two will not allow Khloe or Kalissa out of your sights. I'm searching for a loophole in Zeus's law for me to stay out of the war. Until then, you and the Divinities are free to call on my hounds and any other of my resources." She faced them and stared at Jagger.

His skin tightened, and his heart thumped wildly. The way she'd fixed on him, he guessed she knew he was going to seek out his mother. "Jagger, speak."

"I wish to make a bargain with my mother."

"I see." She glanced to Lex. "Leave us, please."

Lex gave a short nod with his lips pursed. However, his brother knew Jagger would fill him in later. Much later. When Lex dematerialized, Jagger met Hecate's stare. "We don't know which Fate is your mother."

"Then I'll summon all three."

She stepped closer to him and cupped his cheek. The love of a mother lit up her eyes. "You have the power within you to change your own fate. Making deals with the Fates is dangerous. But you are a very stubborn male. Just be careful, and be aware of your surroundings."

Her words circled in his mind. He was a son of the Fates. His powers came from them and his demon father. Understanding settled in with clarity. "I could change fate."

Hecate's eyes went round, and she shook her head. "There is always a price. The balance of the universe must not be disturbed. What you change will have the opposite effect."

"I know, and I will only use the power if I can't keep her alive without it." She frowned, and Jagger shook his head. "I promise to be careful, mother."

She released a sigh and stepped back. "You should return to your mate and stop whatever Khan and his demons are planning."

He gave her a kiss on the cheek and teleported back to the Divinity House. The sight of Khloe peacefully sleeping relaxed him. He would give his own life to ensure that she was safe.

Startled, Khloe rolled over, and her eyes snapped open. She relaxed and smiled at the sight of Jagger lying on his side next to her. Watching her sleep, no doubt.

"Morning."

"Morning." He kissed her forehead, nose, mouth, and down her jawline to her neck.

She moaned as his lips glided over her skin, leaving behind a trail of hot desire. When his warm tongue lapped at her jugular vein, she nearly cried out. The memory of his bite from two nights ago was still etched in her mind, and a stream of lusty need flared straight to her core.

With one hand fisted in his black hair, she tugged and pulled his head up so she could claim his lips. He complied willingly, thrust his tongue into her mouth, and sought hers out in turn. His hand traveled up her outer thigh to her waist and stopped to cup her breast. She arched into his touch, wanting more. No, *needing* more.

He did things to her. Things she didn't completely understand. Not knowing where they were headed or how they would get there scared her. She was addicted to him. There would be no one else, ever.

Oh, gods, I hope my heart doesn't break.

The longer she was with him, the more the wall around her heart crumbled. Before long, Jagger would break through that barrier completely. No. She had to reinforce it. She couldn't be vulnerable, not when they needed to get those children out of Khan's hands and back with their adoptive family.

"Jag," It came out as a breathless whisper, and she cursed herself for the weakness.

He lifted his head, and his dark chocolate eyes met hers. Oh, hell. How was she going to say no to that face? Not to mention the promise of complete bliss in the depths of those eyes.

Giving up on her internal battle between what she shouldn't have and what she wanted, Khloe fisted her hand in his black hair and pulled his lips to hers once more. Jagger met her demand and thrust his tongue inside. She moaned and rubbed her body against his.

The sound of breaking glass in the hallway outside her room made them freeze. A feminine gasp followed by a painful moan spurred Khloe into action. She pushed against Jagger's chest, relieved when he didn't protest. She rushed to the door and yanked it open.

Lydia was doubled over, one hand gripped tightly around the railing and the other placed on the side of her round stomach. Khloe took a step forward but stopped when Jagger gripped her arm.

"Glass." He released her arm, stepped over the broken cup to lift Lydia, and carried her to her room.

Khloe darted after them. By the time they'd reached Lydia's door, Ayden and Kalissa were climbing the stairs. Ayden had his cell phone pressed to his ear. No doubt calling Bethany, Zach's sister and the coven's midwife.

Khloe didn't wait for them. She charged into the room as Jagger laid Lydia on the bed and stepped back. Kneeling at the side of the bed, Khloe laced her fingers with her best friend's. Worry and fear whirled in her gut.

"Something's wrong," Khloe said as Kalissa and Ayden entered the room.

Her brother-in-law leaned over and placed his hand on Lydia's stomach. His sigh of relief and the smile on his face eased Khloe's anxiety a little.

A slight shift of pressure in the room told her Zach had arrived. Khloe briefly looked up and was relieved to see his sister with him.

Bethany went straight into doctor mode. She wasn't technically a doctor but had enough training and experience as the coven's midwife that she was the closest thing they had. "I need everyone out, except Lo and Zach."

"Why me?"

Khloe giggled at the slight terror in Zach's voice.

Beth and Zach stared at each other as if they were having an internal argument, and Khloe knew all too well that's exactly what they were doing. Zach had always been able to communicate telepathically with his immediate family members and now the Divinities, thanks to the bond they all shared.

A few moments later, Zach's shoulders dropped, and he drifted to the opposite side of the bed, sat, and held his hand out to Lydia. "Are you okay with me staying?"

Lydia nodded and curled her fingers around his. Just then, a contraction overtook her, causing her to squeeze Khloe's and Zach's hands.

With her free hand, Khloe conjured a damp wash-cloth and mopped her best friend's forehead. Zach lifted his hand, still linked with Lydia's, and brought it to his lips to place a kiss on her fingers, causing her to focus her gaze on him. Real concern and genuine care wove into his features. He used his empathy to sooth Lydia's emotions, calming her.

Khloe's chest tightened. Jagger entered her thoughts. The way he'd made love to her the night before, ensuring she was pleasured and sated before allowing his own release had torn down the walls around her heart. The poetic words he'd whispered in her ear as he'd thrust deep inside her had made her pulse race as if she were being brought back to life.

It was all too good to be true. She couldn't let her guard down in the hopes that they could make a life together. He'd return to the Afterworld once the children were safe and out of harm's way. So getting attached to the Death Demon was a heartache she didn't need or want.

Another contraction hit Lydia, and she cried out and squeezed Khloe's hand again. "Breathe, Dia. You're doing great."

"Beth, give her something," Zach barked out.

"You know I can't."

The pressure on Khloe's fingers let up, and Lydia started breathing normally again. Khloe scooted onto the bed to be closer to her. Helplessness wrapped around her at seeing her friend in so much pain. Another contraction, and Lydia started to push.

"That's good, Lydia. Hold it." Beth counted to ten. "Okay, rest."

A couple of additional pushes, and the room filled with the cries of a healthy baby boy. Khloe's heart swelled, and tears stung her eyes as Bethany cut the cord, wrapped the wailing infant in a blanket, and placed him on Lydia's chest.

"What will you name him?" Zach whispered while peering down at the bundle in Lydia's arms with a look of awe on his face.

Lydia didn't blink or hesitate with her answer. "Logan Mikal. It's his father's name, flipped around."

Khloe hugged her and pressed the side of her face to her friend's. "It's a beautiful name. Strong."

Khloe held her finger to his hand. Tiny fingers flexed open and closed. That's when she saw his birthmark. Lydia had seen it, too, and she had unwrapped him enough to get a good look at the Divine Rose on the inside of his forearm.

"Oh. He's a Dark Divine," Khloe said with uncertainty in her tone. Logan's rose was a dark red. So dark, it almost looked black. Khloe looked at Lydia, who was equally confused, and smiled. "He'll be safe here. We'll protect him and love him."

Lydia teared up and nodded. "Thanks."

Khloe was unsure how long they sat marveling over the newest and smallest household member before Zach cleared his throat and suggested they leave Lydia to bond with her son.

Khloe reluctantly followed Zach through the bedroom door. She'd have plenty of time to spoil the little guy later.

Jagger leaned against the wall next to the fireplace in the living room, waiting for Khloe and feeling like an outsider. The family togetherness the Divinities shared stirred old feelings of pain and regret. Pain for the loss of his own family, too raw to unbury. Sure, he had Lex and Hecate and loved them both, but the emptiness never left.

Khloe filled that void, offered a sense of belonging. He huffed and pushed off the wall. The irony. He didn't belong anywhere. Not here. Not even in the Afterworld.

He reached the stairs as Khloe stepped off the bottom step, her beautiful face bright with a smile. She took his hand in hers, curling her fingers around his. He let her tug him back into the living room.

"He's perfect." She let go of his hand and sat on the loveseat across from Kalissa and Ayden. "Bethany said she'd bring him down in a bit."

Everyone turned their attention to Jagger. He had a childish urge to disappear. Being the center of attention was one of his most undesirable things.

Jagger returned to his station beside the fireplace. "As you know, Lex and I had a meeting with Hecate. To say she is displeased with the kidnapping of the Dark Divine children would be an understatement. She's furious that Khan would stoop this low. My mother offers whatever services you require. She is bound by Zeus, stopped from having direct involvement, but she's looking into a workaround."

"Hecate didn't share how she would find this loophole, did she?" Zach shrugged at Jagger's raised eyebrow. "It never hurts to ask."

"Tell her we appreciate any help she's able to give." Kalissa snuggled into Ayden.

Jagger studied her for a moment. She looked tired. Her magical signature was slightly duller than usual. It was similar to the way Lydia's aura appeared. Could she be with child?

Kalissa released a sigh. "We were waiting to make an official announcement until I was further along. But considering how things have been going, it's better to get it out in the open. Ayd and I are expecting."

Melaina gasped in surprise. "Congrats, you two. That's wonderful news."

"Thanks. So, I'll be staying at home with Lydia and the baby, but we're not sitting around doing nothing. I expect to be in the loop. Despite what Lo thinks, I *can* work a computer." She looked at her twin and smiled.

Khloe laughed. "I know you can. But I'll still go over some things with you and Lydia first."

A ghostly figure appeared in the center of the living room. Jagger tensed until he realized it was the twins' spirit guide, Barbra.

"The children are not at the warehouse." The ghost floated over to hover in front of Kalissa. "But there are two witches in holding cells in the basement level of the building."

"Witches? Are you sure?"

Barbra turned her head toward him and narrowed her eyes. "If you're asking if they're Divinities, I'm not sure. If they are, their magic is being muted somehow. I didn't hang around taking surveys, demon."

"Barb!" The twins spoke as one, drawing the spirit's attention back to them.

Jagger held up a hand. "It's okay. She's allowed to have her opinion."

"What did the witches look like?" Kalissa asked as

Khloe went to the entertainment center and searched one of the shelves.

"Well, the man had light brown hair. He noticed my presence and peered right at me with irises so pale a blue they were scary. Something primal lay behind those eyes." Barbra shuddered but continued. "The woman had long, red hair and looked a little like your friend, Lydia."

The twins exchanged knowing glances, and Jagger didn't have to be telepathic to know what they were thinking.

Khloe went to stand next to the spirit with a photo in hand. "Is this the woman?"

Barbra studied the picture for a brief moment and nodded. "Yes, that's her."

CHAPTER SEVENTEEN

*H*e sat on a small cot in his dark stone cell with his back and head against the wall, his eyes closed. He didn't dare sleep longer that the ten-minute catnaps he managed. The rest of the time, he sat on the sorry excuse for a bed and listened. He could identify each footstep. He could tell the difference between Demetrius and Paul and distinguish them from the rest of the lowlife demon scum that came down to poke at the tiger in his cage. Let them poke. Eventually, the beast would break out. When it did, they'd better run.

Kristof Rayners wasn't only a Divinity; he was a shifter. Unlike weres, he wasn't ruled by the pull of the moon. His shapeshifter abilities were purely magical. He was able to take more than one form, and always at will unless he was unable to shift. Like now. The collar they'd placed on him kept him from shifting, and his primary beast was getting restless.

The tiger wanted out, and he wanted blood.

The demons talked about a female witch they had locked up on the other side of the building. They called her the blind witch and bragged about how they'd taken her sight with some kind of chemical they'd dropped into her eyes. The news of the creatures torturing a female made Kristof want to rip every one of their heads off their shoulders with his fangs.

He had to find a way out of his cell, find the female, and then find Melaina or Noah. The other Divinities were dead. Except Angelica. She had been missing when he was captured. He just hoped she'd gotten away. He had no idea what had happened to her children, his niece and nephew. Of course, Jacan and Lydia were old enough to take care of themselves, but it was still the thought of them going through the loss of both their parents.

Footsteps coming down the hall toward his cell put his senses on alert. So far, the demons hadn't used force on him. They only came to his cell to bring food. They called it food, at least. Kristof didn't know what it was half the time. He only ate what he recognized and fed the rest to the rats.

The demons stopped outside the door. With a click of the lock, the door opened to reveal Paul and two of the larger demons that always accompanied him. "Get up," Paul demanded. "We're going for a little walk." He motioned to the other demons to take hold of Kirstof.

Paul was afraid him. His fear fragranced the air like a Glade PlugIn. The sweet smell teased his beast. When the demons came to him, he let them take his arms and pull him to a stand. He was curious to see where their little walk would end up. So, he waited like the tiger waits for his prey.

They walked down the hall to where it forked off then turned right and continued down another hall with more cells. Coming to a stop in front of a door halfway down the corridor, one of the demons removed his collar. Kristof tilted his head and smiled. Demons weren't that smart. Yet they seemed to be up to something.

"Getting brave, Paul?" Kristof purred as magic once again raced through his veins. He changed his eyes from human to cat-like and laughed at the fear rolling off Paul. If he had been human, he would have pissed his pants. The door opened, and Kristof froze at the scent he would know anywhere, raising a fear of his own.

Angelica Rayners paced her small cell along the wall so she could feel her way around the room. She had been strong until the day they'd blinded her with that chemical. They had dropped it into her eyes as one of her punishments for not telling them where the Sinew was and how to use it. She put on a good show, but deep down, she was terrified. Scared of what other creative ways they could come up with to persuade her. She just thanked the gods every day that they hadn't raped her. Yet.

She stopped her pacing when footsteps stopped at her door. She breathed in a deep sigh and braced herself for what was coming. It was too early for dinner, so they weren't bringing food. The door opened. She heard the scuffling of feet, and then the door shut and locked. A presence filled the room.

"Who's there?"

"What the fuck did they do to you?"

It came out as a growl, but she would know that voice anywhere. "Kris? Is that you?"

Silence. She feared it was a trick, a ploy to get her to lower her shields.

After a few moments, he spoke, "Yes. You can't see."

She shook her head. "No," she answered softly and shook her head so her hair would hide her face from him. She had scars on her face from the chemicals they'd used to blind her. She hadn't been allowed to heal herself. They kept her in cuffs that bound her powers and prevented her from healing. She stepped forward and reached out to him.

"Please don't come any closer," he said with a shaky tone.

"They haven't allowed you to shift." It wasn't a question. So, this was how it was going to end.

"They took the collar off before shoving me in here. I think they want me to kill you, or scare you."

Kristof paced in front of Angelica. They'd left the lights out. As though it mattered if she couldn't see. Damn bastards. He was so going to enjoy ripping each one of them apart. He would give anything to hold her at that moment. He didn't dare try. His beast wanted more than blood. He wanted sex, and Angelica had always triggered that need. That was the reason he'd left when she'd married his brother, Caleb. They were fated life partners. Kristof couldn't complete with that, so he'd given them their space.

"So change already."

He snapped his head up to look at her. "What?"

"The cameras only pick up video. No sound. Shift, and I will push the call button and make a deal. When they come in…"

"I'm not sure about this, Angie. Once the beast is out, especially after being confined for so long, I can't control it." She knew this. Why was she tempting him?

"I know." She walked toward his voice with her arms out in front of her. "I trust you to keep me safe." She stopped when her fingertips brushed his chest.

He closed the distance between them and turned her around so her back was pressed up against his front. "You know the beast wants more than food," he whispered in her ear. He closed his eyes and hated the fear he caused with that statement. He prayed that they would make it out of there alive.

Kristof released her, and she scrambled to the far wall in search of the call button next to the door. Regrettably, he shifted. Once in tiger form, he let out a roar. She screamed and fumbled her fingers to the intercom.

When she reached it, she pushed and held down the

button. "I'll tell you how to get the Sinew and use it. Please get this animal out of here." She released the button and moved around to put Kristof between her and the door. "I'm cuffed and can't use magic," she whispered.

"Don't worry. I can." Kirstof sent the thought to her.

She relaxed a little and straightened her back. *His brave Angie.*

"We'll get out of here. I promise." Kristof sent the thought to her and shook off the tiger's claim. He couldn't go there.

In tiger form, his night vision was better. He could see only half of her face. There were shadows of scars running down her face like tears. He had to get her out of there and the cuffs off her so she could heal if it wasn't too late. Her magic might erase the physical scars, but her mental ones would not heal with magic. Well, maybe with his mindbender ability, Jacan could take the memories from her and replace them.

The door to the cell opened wide with a loud bang as it crashed into the wall. Kristof whirled around and leapt at the demon that came through the door. He sank his large fangs into the demon's neck and, with a shake, snapped his neck, killing him. Two more demons came through the door. One lunged for him. Kristof killed him with the same ease as the first. Some army Demetrius had. They couldn't even stand up to a tiger.

Angelica screamed. Kristof turned to see another

demon dragging her to the door. Kristof changed back to his human form and willed clothes on at the same time. The demon stopped and stared at him. Kristof laughed. "Yeah, asshole. I can change at will. That is the difference between weres and witch-shifters. Let her go and I'll make your death quick."

"Don't kill me. I can get you out of here," the young demon said with real fear in his voice.

"How can I trust you? I let you live, and you go to your superior. I don't think so."

Kirstof raised his hands toward the demon. "Wait! I know what they had planned for you. I know how to stop him." The demon released his hold on Angelica and helped her steady herself. "I'm sorry, miss." The demon touched her face, and the scars lightened. Then he brushed his fingers over the cuff on her wrist, and it too vanished.

"Why are you helping us?" Kirstof asked, still not trusting the demon.

"I am dead either way. You kill me, or Demetrius kills me for failing." The demon shrugged. "This way, I have a chance."

Angelica reached out for Kristof. "Kris, Ryn is the only one who refused to hurt me."

Kristof took Angelica's outstretched hand, drew her to him, and turned a piercing glare on the demon. "How did you manage that without getting killed?"

"My main responsibilities are surveillance. Who do you think gave them the idea to put you with her? I told them that you were half were and couldn't control the beast." Ryn smiled and shook his head. "They can be stupid when they get desperate. We should be going before Demetrius and Paul return." He looked down at the dead demons on the floor. "He may reanimate them to get information."

Kristof created a fireball in his hand and flung it toward the bodies on the floor. The bodies went up in a *poof* like charcoal soaked with lighter fluid and lit with a match.

"You will pledge your allegiance to Hecate?" When the demon nodded, Kristof said, "We'll see." He walked out the door and up the hall while holding Angelica's hand, Ryn close on his heels. Once on the ground floor above the basement where they'd been imprisoned, Kristof teleported the three of them out of there.

CHAPTER EIGHTEEN

Khloe sat at the kitchen island, tapping her foot against the base of the barstool. Her mind whirled with the confirmation of the whereabouts of Angelica Rayners. She was so close. Intuition had told her that warehouse was more than it appeared.

Now they had two rescue missions, and Lydia, her new bestie, would have her mother back. A lump formed in Khloe's throat, and a tinge of jealousy rose. No, she would not be envious of Lydia. She of all people deserved good news.

"We can't say anything to her."

Khloe cut her gaze to Kalissa. "She has a right to know."

"Not right now. She's been through too much and is now healing from childbirth. Give her a few days."

Nodding, Khloe propped her elbow on the countertop to rest her chin in her palm and watched Zach cut up veggies for omelets. The sight made her smile. The man loved to cook, almost more than he loved to chase bad guys. He didn't care what species he was chasing either.

The demons were the worst out there.

"We have to find the children. I think they should be our priority," Zach said without breaking his veggie-chopping rhythm.

"So Angelica and Kristof are left to fend for themselves?" The words jetted out more furious than she'd intended.

"They are adults. We know where they are, and we know they're alive."

"He's right," Kalissa's agreed. "We can't go charging into the warehouse. The demons may, in turn, harm the children. We can't risk it."

Khloe growled in frustration. "We don't know where they are."

Mel sat a cup of coffee in front of her. "Angie and Kris are fighters and very strong. In fact, I wouldn't put it past Kris to be planning something. He's not the type to sit and wait."

Light footsteps came up from behind, keeping Khloe from asking another question. Swiveling the stool around, she smiled. Bethany held little Logan in her arms, wrapped up like a burrito in a blue blanket. She stopped next to Khloe, who peeked at the tiny face showing out of the blanket.

"He's perfect." Khloe lifted her eyes and met Beth's. "I miss Cassia when she was this small."

Kalissa appeared next to them. "Can I hold him?"

"Sure." Bethany handed off Logan, instructing Kalissa on how to support his head.

A familiar warmth enclosed Khloe from behind, followed by Jagger's arms around her waist. She leaned back and breathed in his sandalwood scent. When his lips touched her temple, she closed her eyes, enjoying the connection, the feel of him. She lifted her hand, touched his cheek, and froze.

Pulsating energy thumped on her skin, but it wasn't from the growing bond between her and Jagger. The wards around the property were going off. Everyone except Jagger and Bethany felt it.

Zach rushed around the counter and ushered Kalissa and Beth out of sight. Khloe bolted off the stool and marched straight for the front door. Ayden and Mel were one step ahead of her.

Jagger gripped her wrist, halting her. "What's going on?"

"The wards are going off. A demon has entered the property." She twisted out of his grasp and exited the house.

Rumbling along the ground like the sounds of a stampede made her smirk. Teddy-Bear stormed to the front of the line. With a flash of light, they were two separate hellhounds instead of the Siamese twins they'd been born as.

A few moments later, three bodies emerged from the tree line to the left of the driveway. The magical energy that pulled at Khloe's own signature told her two were Divinities. The third was a demon, and the reason the wards went off.

Mel let out a sob. "Angelica? Kris?"

She stepped forward toward the trio. Khloe and the others filed in behind her. The demon shifted nervously at Kristof's side.

"Who's the demon?"

Kris meet Khloe's gaze. "I'd ask you the same thing." His gaze shifted to peer at Jagger. Khloe stepped in front her demon. That got a crooked grin from Kris. "But I know there are only two Death Demons alive, and they're loyal only to Hecate."

Jagger stepped forward, pressing his hard body into hers as if hearing an undercurrent of threat in Kris's tone.

Mel cleared her throat. "Kris, do explain your demon."

After a few seconds, his shoulders eased, and he twined his fingers with Angelica's. "This is Ryn. He helped us escape, and I thought he could be useful. He's very much aware that he dies the minute he betrays us."

Out of the three of them, it was Angelica she studied briefly, noting the faint scars that streamed down her face and the blank stare in her sea-green eyes. The damn demons had blinded her.

Khloe shifted her attention to the stranger with

them. The demon lowered his head like a servant. Which he was. His power level was that of the lowest Khloe had felt in a *Lackey* before, almost muted. The perfect slave to his demon master, unable to fight back. Khloe couldn't help the small amount of pity that rose in her chest.

"Ryn, these are the Divinities. Well, some of them."

"Let's go inside. Zach was making breakfast." Khloe turned toward the house. Teddy-Bear had rejoined and shrunk back to the size of a two-headed Rottweiler. Teddy nuzzled her hand. She stroked his fur. "Keep your eyes on that demon."

She bounded up the steps and entered the living room as Zach and Kalissa waited by the stairs. Khloe had opened her mind to her twin and telepathically let her know what was happening.

While breakfast was being prepared, they filled Angelica and Kris in on Demetrius and the Sinew. When Angelica asked about her children, everyone fell silent. It was Kalissa who spoke. Khloe was grateful, too.

"Well, you have a beautiful, healthy grandson. Lydia gave birth a few hours ago, and she's upstairs resting."

"And Jacen?"

The hopefulness and longing in Angelica's voice broke Khloe's heart. This time, it was Ayden who stepped forward. He knelt down in front of where she sat on the sofa and took her hands to bring them to his face. "It's Ayden. Todd's son."

A smile lifted her lips, and she moved her fingers over his face. "You're all grown up." Then she frowned. "I'm sorry about your parents."

Ayden took her hands in his again and spoke softly. "Jacen…made a sacrifice. He risked his life to save mine. I'm so sorry."

Angelica fell silent and slid her hands from Ayden's. "Ang—"

She shook her head and held up her hand. "I want to freshen up and see Lydia and the baby."

"I'll take you up." Kalissa came around and took Angie's elbow.

After the women had left the room, Kris asked, "So do you know what Demetrius is up to?"

"We believe Khan is raising an army with the Dark Divine. The bastard, Demetrius, even stooped low enough to taking the children." Khloe didn't bother to rein in her emotions. Thunder rumbled over the house.

From the corner of the living room, sitting at the desk, Ryn broke his silence. "I know where the children are."

CHAPTER NINETEEN

*J*agger followed Khloe as she rushed up the stairs to her room. Jagger stood propped against the doorframe, watching her sensual form fly around the room as she gathered clothes to shove inside a duffel bag. She grabbed her laptop and case. "Do you always go off half-cocked?"

Teal eyes met his, and she smiled. "Yes, I do. It's how I get things done." She moved past him, making sure her hip brushed his growing erection. *Tease.* He would pay her back for that the first chance he got. With a low growl, he followed her down the stairs.

"Zach, Mel, and I will be about ten minutes behind you. That way, we're not obvious and don't alert them that we know something. I'm sure they're still watching the house," Ayden said as he came out of his and Kalissa's bedroom.

Jagger nodded then pointed to Ryn. "You're with us."

Khloe said she knew where the farmhouse was where Ryn claimed the children had been taken. It was only an hour drive from the Divinity House. Plenty of time to press the *Lackey* for more information.

Five minutes later, they were buckled up and on the road.

"What did you do for Demetrius?"

The demon's head snapped in Jagger's direction then to the rearview mirror to look at Khloe. "I ran computer surveillance and security."

"No shit!"

Jagger laughed, knowing full well what Khloe's outburst meant. "Then you'll know the layout of the farmhouse and how to get in."

Ryn nodded.

"Lighten up. You just bought yourself more time to live." Jagger let out another chuckle and looked at Khloe's amused expression.

"What's wrong with your powers?"

Silence invited Jagger to peer into the backseat to see a confused look on the demon's face. "Your powers are…weak."

"Demetrius gives us a serum that weakens our magic. It doesn't work on Divinities, and he's trying to make one that does; at least he was before I helped the only two he had escape." A gleeful grin spread across Ryn's face.

"Dude, you're screwed," Khloe said with a laugh.

Jagger held in his amusement. "How long until the serum wears off and you gain your strength back?"

Ryn shrugged. "I managed to skip the last dosage two days ago. Another day, and I'll begin to regain my powers, but don't worry, I'm full-blooded *Lackey*."

Khloe snorted. "I've fought a few *Lackeys,* and they not all that weak."

"You fought the scouts. Demetrius—"

Jagger held up his hand. "Let me guess. The scouts are given a serum to boost their powers."

"Nice. The worker bees get shafted while the soldiers get power boosts."

Jagger raised a brow at the pity in her tone, but he let go. They rode the rest of the way in silence.

Khloe pulled over a block past the farmhouse and parked on the shoulder. She scanned their surroundings. "Everything's quiet."

Turning her gaze to Jagger, she watched as a lazy smile lifted his sensual lips, and he stretched his large, muscular frame. Khloe suppressed the urge to run her hands down his body. Hell, forget the hands. She wanted her tongue to do the roaming.

She gasped in surprise when he captured her mouth with his, his tongue slipping inside, searching. Warmth pooled between her legs, and her panties dampened.

A tap on her window startled both of them. She twisted around ready to hurl a fireball at someone. Ryn stood outside the car, arms folded over his chest, and a smirk on his face. Damn demon.

Khloe removed her seatbelt and climbed out of the car. Once Jagger was at her side, they crossed the road and walked into the woods. The farmhouse was surrounded by wards. No surprise there. She didn't consider any other option. She just wanted to get close enough to the house to get a visual. With Ryn, they had their map.

Stopping at a break in the trees right before the magical barrier that served as an alarm system, she saw the two-story farmhouse. It was about half the size of her family home, but it was cute. A wrap-around front porch with white columns on either side of the front door added to the family appeal.

"The children are kept in a room in the basement."

Ryn's voice was way too close to her. With her index finger, she poked him in the shoulder and pushed. He took the hint and moved. Jagger chuckled beside her. She rolled her eyes and headed back to the Lexus.

Ten minutes later, they sat in the living room of a two-bedroom suite. Ayden had booked two suites side-by-side. Khloe's laptop was open, and with Ryn's guidance and knowledge, she was surfing Demetrius's security system. It took all the fun out of breaking in, but it was much quicker to use the password.

When they found the layout of the farmhouse, she plugged the laptop into the TV, using it as a secondary monitor so everyone could see the images.

"Ryn said the kids are kept in the basement."

The demon bobbed his head. "There's a room down there with a bed, refrigerator, and bathroom."

If he was trying to reassure her that the children were provided for, he did a lousy job of it. "It sounds like a cell to me." She clutched her hands into tight balls and tried not to lash out. He was trying to help.

Jagger covered one of her fists, and she relaxed her hand and allowed his fingers to link with hers. His warmth and power cradled her. She'd never been one to depend on someone for support, but with Jagger, she wanted to let down her guard and allow him inside. Their gazes locked, and for a brief moment, that's all she wanted.

As if picking up on her shift in focus, Ayden cleared his throat. "We'll go at sundown. Ryn, can you get us past the wards?"

"Not a problem."

The meeting broke with everyone going to their areas of the rooms. Khloe was glad for the break.

Although she wanted to get the kids away from the demons and safe at home as soon as possible, she needed some private time with Jagger. They had to discuss their future—if they had one.

She picked up her duffel bag and strode to the nearest bedroom. Jagger entered a few seconds later and shut the door behind him. He came up behind her and wrapped his arms around her waist. Brushing her hair aside, he placed a soft kiss on her neck.

She'd promised herself she would never feel this again, never trust another with her heart. Now it was too late. Jagger had stolen it.

His fingers traveled up her arms to her shoulders. Desire roared in her veins like a fiery tidal wave.

"I've been waiting to get you alone."

Jagger's growled confession in her ear sent the fiery wave straight to her core. She pressed her back into his front with a moan and slid her hands up the sides of his legs and around to his ass. Another growl followed by a hiss came from Jagger, making Khloe smile in satisfaction at his arousal.

When one of his strong arms snaked around her waist and held her in place, she lost any control she'd hoped to have. But, she was okay with it. The sense of peace and the promise of complete bliss allowed her to lower her guard and submit to his demands.

CHAPTER TWENTY

*G*ods, this woman drove him mad. Everything about her pushed Jagger further over the edge of sanity with each passing moment. He feared he would never get enough of her, never be able to let her go.

He drew in her scent as he glided his hands down her stomach to the hem of her T-shirt and tugged it over her head. She shifted as if to turn around, but he stopped her. Her pulse picked up, but it wasn't out of fear. It was in anticipation of what he would do to her.

Khloe's desire drifted over him, caressed and enticed him. With her back pressed to his front, he lightly slid his fingers over the soft skin of her arms. She shuddered and released a barely audible sigh. He buried his nose in her neck, relishing her natural chocolate-rose scent. She was his, and he wanted to possess every inch of her.

Walking her forward to stand in front of the dresser and mirror, he suppressed a growl at the sight of their reflections. Khloe in nothing but her blue jeans and white lace bra and him fully dressed.

"You're beautiful." He touched her cheek with his lips and moved to her ear. She didn't respond. Her teal eyes held his while her hands wrapped around to grip his ass, pressing their bodies tighter together.

Closing his eyes, Jagger regained control over the mounting need inside him. When he opened his lids, he cursed. Khloe had removed her jeans by magic. Half of her sensual mouth lifted in a smirk as she rotated her hips against the stiffening erection behind his zipper.

He placed his hands on her hips, halting her torturous teasing. Holding her still with one hand, he moved the other down beneath the waistband of her panties. When his fingers slid between her slick folds, she sucked in a breath. Upon her exhale, she released a whimper and melted into him.

Khloe braced her hands on the dresser and moved with his strokes. Jagger entered her with one finger then two. He watched as she rode him, closed her eyes, and threw back her head. Each movement she made drove him closer to his own release. Her bottom rubbed over his hard cock still confined behind denim.

"Let go, Khloe," he growled and kissed her cheek and trailed kisses to her neck. "Come for me. I want to feel you come unglued."

Her walls clenched his fingers as he pumped in and out of her while his thumb caressed her clit. Her little pants became heavier and more frequent until she released a muffled scream as an orgasm overtook her.

When the last shudder rolled through Khloe's body, she melted into Jagger. It was a good thing he still held on to her. He withdrew his hand from between her thighs and she went to turn around, only to be stopped with his hands on her hips.

His lips brushed against her ear, his warm breath caressing her cheek, sending tiny prickles over her skin. "Don't move."

The growled demand sent a hot, wild need straight to her sex, and she groaned and ground her ass into his jean-covered cock. A hiss escaped his lips, and his grip on her hips tightened. Grinning, she reached back to unbutton his pants.

"Khloe."

It was a warning, and it made her giggle. Gods, she

hadn't felt this giddy in a very long time. Not since before her parents had died, and even longer...before Mark had ripped her heart out. Closing her eyes, she pushed the uninvited, dark thoughts away and focused on Jagger. He grounded her in a way she didn't think possible.

Damn. She was falling in love.

"Khloe?"

She lifted her hand to his head and slid her fingers into his short, black hair. "I'm fine. Just make it so my thoughts don't wander. And lose the pants."

A chuckle vibrated through her as he said, "Yes, ma'am."

"That's better."

She gasped at the feel of his hard length, bare against her rump, his jeans and her panties now gone. Damn, he was fast. She didn't even sense him use his magic. It wasn't the first time, either. They'd have to talk about that, she decided.

Jagger ran his hand up her back, gently pushing her upper body until she was bent forward. With his knee, he nudged her legs apart. Bracing her hands on the dresser, she watched him in the mirror. When he slid inside her, all reason and most of her sanity evaporated from her. She managed to keep her eyes open and locked with Jagger's, now laced with sparks of crimson. His fangs poked out from behind his lips, and she shivered at the memory of them piercing her skin. Would he bite her again?

He picked up his pace with each thrust, sending them both further over the edge until they came together.

CHAPTER TWENTY-ONE

*H*e was perfect.

From his ten toes and ten fingers to the auburn fuzz on the top of his head, Logan Mikal was Lydia's blessing in the darkest part of her life. Burying her father and then her husband two years later had broken her heart. The pain never subsided. And when Jacen had sacrificed himself to save Ayden a little over a month ago, something inside her had snapped.

The lives of her family would not go unavenged. Once she healed, she would work out and get back in shape. Then the demons would pay for every sin. It was the least she could do.

A light tap on her door halted her dark musings. "Come in."

The door slowly opened, and Kalissa entered. She hovered near the door, a whirlwind of emotions playing on her face. "Good, you're awake. How's Logan?"

Lydia smiled and peered down at her sleeping son. His lips made a suckling motion. "He's perfect."

"How are you feeling?"

Lydia's suspicion turned to alarm. "What happened? Is it the Dark Divine children?"

Kalissa released a soft laugh. "No. We've found their location. The others should be at the Georgia border by now."

Relieved that the children were going to be rescued reduced only some of the worry Lydia felt at Kalissa's strange behavior. Through the Divinity bond Hecate had placed on them, Lydia felt Lis's uneasiness. She shifted from foot to foot and looked back at the open door every few seconds.

"Lis, what is it?"

The blonde Divinity dropped her shoulders and took a couple of steps forward. "I have news about your mother and uncle."

Lydia's chest tightened, and her sight blurred.

Kalissa advanced toward her, shaking her head, and sat on the bed next to her. "Don't cry. They're alive. And here."

It took several moments before the words sank in. Her mother was alive and here? In this house? Footsteps drew her attention to the door. She gasped at the sight of her mother being led in by Kristof. Tears streamed down her face, but they were quickly replaced with anger as her uncle and mother got closer.

The ugly, faded scars running down her mother's cheeks, and the way she clung to Kris as he led her toward the bed only added to the anger building inside Lydia. She grabbed Kalissa's hand, drawing her attention. "What is wrong with her?" It was barely audible, but the other witch heard her nonetheless. She shook her head in a silent plea to stay calm.

Kalissa stood, making room for Angelica to sit in her place. Lydia met Kris's gaze when he bent down to kiss her on the forehead. When he hugged her, he whispered, "She's been through hell." He drew back and locked his eyes with hers. "Gods, I've missed you." Lydia opened her mouth to speak, but he shook his head. "We'll catch up later. Right now is mother/daughter time."

Kalissa and Kris left the room, shutting the door behind them.

Angelica reached out. Lydia took her hand and brought it to her face. "Mom, what did they do to you?"

"Shhh. The only thing that matters now is that I'm here."

Lydia wanted to argue. She wanted to know what those monsters had done. She wanted them all to pay. Taking a deep breath, she calmed the building rage and focused on the fact that her mother was alive and sitting in front of her.

Her son squirmed and whimpered. Lydia smiled

and cooed to the little man in her arms. "Mom, I want you to meet your grandson, Logan." Lydia guided Angelica's hand to the restless baby.

A beautiful smile lit up her mother's face when she touched Logan. She ran her hand over him, studying his small form with her fingers. Lydia then shifted her son to place him in Angelica's arms.

"Oh, Dia, I don't think that is a good idea."

"Sure it is." Lydia leaned into her mother and placed a kiss over each eye then cupped her face. "I wish you sight, if only for tonight. Blessed Be." Drawing back, she frowned when nothing changed in Angelica's eyes. She released a sigh and sat back. "I'm sorry. I thought I had enough juice left to heal some of your sight."

Her mother shook her head. "It did help. The dark shadows are clearer. I can see." She laughed and peered down at her grandson, now sleeping peacefully in her arms. "Everything is fuzzy, but I can see."

Lydia found it hard to keep her eyes off the woman she'd feared she would never see again. It was all so surreal that her mother was alive and holding her grandson. No matter how many times Lydia had imagined and dreamed of this day, it still seemed so unreal. "Mom, what happened...with Dad?"

Not taking her gaze off Logan, Angie answered, "It was the first snowfall, and your father and I took a walk. He said he was going to build me the biggest snowman anyone had ever seen." She lifted her head. The tears Lydia was holding back, slid down her cheeks at the loss in her mother's eyes. Before she could ask her to continue, Angie began speaking again. "When we reached the old bridge, a current of dark magic hung thickly in the air. A few moments later, a dark figure appeared. Your father shoved me behind him just as the creature shot a lethal energy bolt at us. It happened too fast. Once your father was hit, another creature snatched me from behind and dragged me away."

Lydia rested a hand on her mother's arm, silencing her. Logan was stirring again. "We'll hold a remembrance ceremony for all who've been lost. For Father, Jacen, the Danielses, and the Bradentons."

Angelica's tear-filled gaze met hers, and she nodded. "That would be nice."

"Right now, we have a new life to celebrate. Two, in fact." The puzzled look on her mother's face made her laugh. "Logan's and yours. We could have a slumber party in here since I'm supposed to be on bed rest for the next day or so."

"That sounds great."

Relief washed through Lydia at the lightened mood and the chance to act somewhat normal for a little while. "Oh, and wait until you meet Teddy-Bear."

Khloe and Jagger were the first to materialize about fifty feet away from the magical barrier surrounding the farmhouse. A creepy, dark visage fell over the old house as the sun set behind it. Shadows seemed to come out of nowhere.

"An illusion spell," Khloe mused aloud.

"It keeps humans away."

Khloe rolled her eyes at Ryn's voice behind her. She knew that, and sure didn't need the *Lackey* to state the obvious. Instead of showing her irritation, though, she let it go. Ignoring the demon was best. For now.

She held her hand out, palm up, for one of the two devices Ryn and she had worked on earlier. To the untrained eye, they looked like metal boxes the size of her palm. Inside each box was a spell mixed with hers and the demon's magic.

When cool metal touched her hand, she pivoted to her right to find the weakest point in the wards. Sometimes, if the circle wasn't closed completely when the magical barrier was set, a vulnerable spot was left behind. Gods, she hoped there was one.

After a few steps, she stopped, straightened her back, and whirled around. Ryn jerked back a step. Khloe rolled her eyes and pointed behind him. "Go that way with Ayden and Zach. Mel, Jag, and I will go this way."

Ryn quickly turned around and trotted after Ayd and Zach. She shook her head and continued around the perimeter. Jagger fell back in beside her. "Don't say anything. I still don't trust the little shit."

The sound of his chuckle spiked her desire, and she watched him as he took two strides to fall in line in front of her. Broad, muscular shoulders rolled and flexed with every step. Her eyes followed one arm down to his hand, and she shuddered at the memory of what those hands had done to her earlier.

"Lo, focus." Jagger's teasing tone only made her want him more.

Damn demon.

But he was right. She had to focus. After the children were safe at Maxville Coven, she'd have plenty of time for naughty thoughts and actions.

She took a few more steps before Mel called out, "It's here."

Khloe turned toward the other Divinity. Melaina waved her hand in a side-to-side motion. Ripples formed on the magical barrier, making it temporarily visible. A flutter of hope and excitement ran through Khloe.

Thank the gods.

The weakness in the wards would buy them some time, not much, but enough to at least get to the children.

Khloe's connection to all elements warned her just before Ryn, Ayden, and Zach materialized beside them. Whispers from the air spirits in the wind had told her who was coming.

"Are you in my head again, Ayd?" She sent her brother-in-law a teasing smile.

He chuckled. "Always. It's such an entertaining place to be."

"The ripples went around to the other side of the wall like a wave," Khloe said, explaining what Ayden had seen.

"Now who's in whose head?"

She laughed and gave a shrug. They were still adjusting to the bond that had forged Ayden, Kalissa, and Khloe together a month ago. The triple connection was both a blessing and a curse. There were things about Ayden Khloe could live without knowing, but they were working on building mental shields to give each other some privacy.

Khloe held out her metal box and waited for Ryn to step up beside her with his. Taking a deep breath, she drew strength from the air and earth around her. She might go off half-cocked sometimes, well, most of the time, but she never played when it came to magic. Especially with a spell she'd never performed before and one that was mixed with demon magic.

She wanted to let the *Lackey* perform the spell while she was safe behind the shield Zach had just put up around the others. But she wasn't a coward, and according to Ryn, the only way to lower the wards without detection was to have both white and black magic.

Gods, she hated messing with black magic. She said a short blessing for this spell to harm no one.

"I'm ready," she said, giving Ryn the go-ahead.

Together, they opened each box and held them straight out, as close to the wards' wall as they could get without touching it. They softly spoke the incantation to invoke the spell. It wasn't a fancy phrase like most would think. No, just one randomly chosen word of Latin that Ryn had picked out, one that loosely translated to open.

The demon wasn't very creative.

From her box, a white cloud of smoke floated up and drifted toward the black smoke that came from Ryn's box. The light and dark magic twined together until they became one gray magical cloud. Khloe called upon the wind to gently blow the energy into the wards, and the cloud disappeared.

The weak point of the wall discolored, making it completely visible, and continued around in both directions to meet on the other side of the perimeter. Worry started to settle in. What if the demons could see it?

A few seconds later, the wards disappeared. The surge of magical energy was gone.

She stood there, listening, waiting for an attack, but it didn't come.

Behind her, Zach's circle fell. Everything went silent. The hum of power from the wards and Zach's shield no longer electrified the air. No lights illuminated the yard around the farmhouse.

The calm before the storm.

Creepy.

"Should I be worried that demons didn't charge out of the house?" Khloe's pulse quickened. Something felt off. This was too easy.

"They won't notice for a little while. We should have enough time to get to the children." Ryn stepped forward and crossed the spot where the magical wall had once been.

She looked behind her and met Ayden's gaze. Yep, he felt it, too.

Jagger stepped to her left side. Ayden moved to her right and took her elbow in a gentle hold. She stared into his baby-blue eyes and frowned.

"Be very careful. Nothing will be as it seems. Think before you react."

Huh?

"What did you see?" Peering into Ayden's concerned gaze, images slammed into her mind. Samoan's evil smile never faltered as she lunged forward to stab Khloe with something. Burning pain rushed through her blood but vanished in an instant when Ayden let go of her and stepped back.

What the fuck?

She'd picked up visions from Kalissa before, but not since she'd bonded with Ayden. They were never as vivid as the one she'd just shared with her brother-in-law. There was only one possibility; he'd pushed the vision on her.

Khloe pushed past him and marched across the yard to the back of the house. Taking deep breaths, she calmed herself. She really needed to get a grip. Ayden was only showing her the vision as a warning, and the information was good to have. One, it meant Samoan —a.k.a. she-demon-bitch—was inside that farmhouse. Two, Khloe would get her chance for payback. She owed the demonic elf an ass kicking for both Kalissa's kidnapping a couple of months before and the abduction of the Dark Divine children.

Jagger's earthy sandalwood scent enveloped her as he fell into step with her. Taking a deep breath, she pulled in the familiar, comforting smell. "Please, don't say it."

His deep chuckle warmed her to her core, and she almost groaned aloud. "I can wait."

With a shake of her head and an eye roll, she stopped, took his hands in hers, and met his intense gaze. "*We* are getting those kids out. Together." She snaked her fingers through his short black hair, pulled his head to hers, and kissed him deeply.

His arms wrapped around her, eliminating the empty space between them. With his hand fisted in her hair, he pulled her head back. "Be very careful."

Jagger released her and walked toward the farm-house, leaving her breathless and needy. Damn demon.

Samoan stormed into the security center after receiving a call from her very pissed-off father. Seriously? Did Demetrius really think she knew how the Divinities had escaped? She wasn't their keeper or nursemaid. In fact, she hated being around the witches. If it were up to her, she would have gotten rid of them a long-ass time ago instead of playing with them like a couple of lab rats.

So, did she care if they'd left? Hell, no. Good riddance.

But what did bother her was they'd taken Ryn with them. The little shit would spill everything he knew and, most likely, lead them straight to where she'd hidden the Dark Divine.

Damn it. Why did she always have to clean up after people and fix others' fuckups?

The door to the lab opened, and she didn't need to turn around to know who it was. The pure evil, pissed-at-the-world power slammed into her. She had to fight a gasp because there was no showing weakness to her father. It was your one-way ticket to hell.

She might be his natural-born daughter, but that didn't mean he'd spare her life any more than the other lowlifes around here. He'd struck her down many times as an example to the others. Rule with fear. That was Demetrius.

"I need a way to make those witches pay," she spat before he stepped into her personal space. "They will pay..."

Her father's gaze shifted to the computer center to her left. Slowly, she turned to see a red light flash on the control panel.

"What is that?"

His lips twitched and rose into a smirk. "They just crossed over the perimeter of the farmhouse."

With arms crossed, she narrowed her eyes. "How do you know that?"

"Liam installed underground electronic sensors around the property."

She wasn't convinced. "Wouldn't Ryn know about those?"

He shrugged and moved to the computer. "I never got around to giving him the access code."

Amazing. For once, her father's laziness had paid off.

"So the little shit led them into a trap." She pivoted toward the door and stopped halfway when he called her name.

He came to her, took her hand, and placed a syringe full of a yellowish liquid into it. She peered up into his face when he spoke. "The Bradenton twins carry the were gene. Their father was half wereleopard. This is an enhancer I've been working on. Inject a small amount into each of them. The change will happen hard and fierce. It'll drive them insane."

"And they will turn on everyone."

"Yes. I am tired of playing nice with those witches."

It was about time he saw it her way. She closed her fingers around the needle and tucked it inside the sheath strapped to her right thigh. Standing on her toes, she kissed him on the cheek.

Before she got to the door, her father said, "Don't fail me, Samoan."

Clenching her teeth together, she yanked the door open and stepped outside.

Love you too, Daddy.

CHAPTER TWENTY-TWO

*C*rouching below a small window, Khloe waited for Ayden and demon boy to catch up. Ayd had stayed behind with Ryn to reset the wards.

Zach shifted uncomfortably beside her. "It's too damn quiet."

Yes, she'd noticed that, too. Even she felt the shift in the air as the wards fell. She expected someone to at least stick their head out the door in curiosity. But, nothing. "I agree. It feels like a trap. The *Lackey* has some explaining to do."

"It would be just like Demetrius to have a backup and not share it with Ryn." Melaina's cool tone was barely audible.

She had a point. Khloe hoped for Ryn's sake that was the case. She was starting to warm to the demon. If he betrayed them, she would kill him herself.

Jagger's hand covered hers, soothing her impulse to

charge into that house, firing first, asking questions later. His all-too-familiar strength and power wrapped around her. She turned her hand over to link her fingers with his. Giving his hand a little squeeze, she asked the group, "Ready?"

Everyone nodded and, in single file, crept along the wall of the house to the back door. Ryn had said the children were being held in the basement. So the back door was the logical place to go in. The blueprints of the farmhouse indicated that the entrance to the cellar was off the kitchen, which was adjacent to the back door.

The plan was to go in and grab the kids without detection. In a perfect world, that would work. This wasn't a perfect world, and these were demons they were dealing with. Demonic beings with supernatural hearing and strength.

Khloe was ready for the charge as they opened the back entrance, only to be highly disappointed when no stood on the other side. Not good. "I don't like this." So what were they doing? Playing poker, watching a football game? She wanted to scream, call out to the bastards that they were here.

Ayden leaned in to whisper in her ear. "Zach, Ryn, and I will get the children. You and the others search the house."

"Those fuckers are up to something, and I want to be able to get the kids out of here before the shit flies."

Khloe smiled at Ayden's telepathic statement. She loved her brother-in-law.

Advancing toward the living room with Jagger and Mel close behind her, she flexed her fingers and opened her senses to the elements. Power filled her from head to toe, energizing her. When they entered the room, no one was there. Strange. Where the hell was everyone?

"This smells too much like a trap," Khloe said through her teeth. Cowards. All of them.

It wasn't smart for the Underworld scum to make her wait. Her patience was running very thin. Breaking glass came from the kitchen. Fear for the children burned in the pit of her stomach. Instinctually, Jagger and Mel flashed to the other room. But, something held Khloe in place. Something was very wrong. She tried to teleport, but she couldn't.

What the fuck?

Screw it. She took a step to join the others as they rushed toward the back of the house but froze when two very large demons stepped into her path. Hairless heads sat atop broad, muscular shoulders. Their skin possessed a purple hue. Silver hieroglyphics, which she didn't recognize, stuck out from under the black tees hugging their chests.

Good color choice in clothing. It matched their dark aura.

"You boys looking for a good time?" She laughed at their confused looks. *Poor things. They've been deprived of humor. Too bad they won't live long enough to find out what they've been missing.*

With a flick of her hands toward the creepo-brothers, she released the energy she'd built up when entering the living room. The magical orb hit an invisible wall and bounced back at her. She twisted out of the way, but she wasn't fast enough. Searing pain hit her in the back and knocked her to the ground. Stunned, she tried to catch her breath and will herself to move before those bastards reached her.

Whatever was keeping her from teleporting also slowed her down. The air felt thick, as though she were trying to walk against the wind in a hurricane, and that feeling wasn't from the energy blast she'd just taken. There was something else, someone else controlling the magic in the room. Only one being possessed the power to do that. An elf, and not just any elf.

Samoan.

Rolling to her side, Khloe reached for the sofa and pulled herself to a stand. She glared at Samoan's smiling face. Her blue-black hair was pulled back in a ponytail, revealing her pointed ears. Those cobalt-blue eyes were a little darker than normal. The demoness wore leather pants and a black tank top that put her full breasts on display.

Khloe rolled her eyes, straightened to her full height of five-nine, and glared at Samoan. "It's not a pleasure to see you, Samoan."

"Aw. It's a pity you say that, Khloe. Because I am

happy to see you. Where is your sister? It's not a party without both of you." Samoan's sweet smile made Khloe want to hurl.

Fake bitch. What the hell was she up to?

The vision Ayden had shared with her flashed briefly in her mind. There was something there that she'd missed. It was a given that Samoan wanted to kill her, but what else?

The demonic elf shifted a step to her left, bringing Khloe's focus back to her. Samoan's hand rested beside the blade strapped to her leg. So, that's how she wanted to play?

Khloe conjured a knife and returned a smile of her own. The male demons, who moved to stand behind Samoan, inched closer in a weak attempt to protect their leader. Samoan held her hand up to stop them. They obeyed like well-trained animals.

Suddenly antsy, Khloe pushed down the urge to charge forward and pound the shit out of the she-demon. She needed to stay focused and think about her options. Because, according to the vision, Samoan was going to kill her.

That was one thing she couldn't let happen. She had a mission and, for the first time in five years, a future. She'd be damned if Samoan was going to take that away from her.

Samoan advanced on her suddenly, unexpectedly. Khloe ducked her swinging fist and punched her in the stomach. She staggered back a step but quick recovered and charged back at Khloe again. This time, the female demon made contact. Both of them hit the ground and rolled until Samoan pinned her.

A sharp prick in her hip made Khloe gasp. A spit second later, her veins felt like someone had shot lava into her. As the fire raced through her bloodstream, each joint ached as though they were being pulled apart.

"What the fuck did you do to me, bitch?" Khloe growled out, finding it hard to catch her breath.

Samoan let out an evil, much-too-satisfied laugh. "Your father was part were. Now you will be one."

Then she vanished, taking her demon guards with her.

Khloe couldn't think. The pain was too much. Every bone felt as though it were breaking. With every breath, she screamed in agony until darkness overtook her.

Jagger twisted the neck of the last demon in the room and let the lifeless body drop to the floor. Zach had managed to get the kids out the back door and, hopefully, was waiting in the van they'd rented earlier that day.

Looking at Ayden and Mel, he asked, "You two okay?"

Ayden nodded. "Yeah. Thanks."

Where was Khloe? Her scream brought the answer.

Heart stopping, he fought to breathe as fear flooded him. He flashed from the back of the house to the living room. But, he didn't see the Khloe he recognized. A black leopard with the same magical signature as Khloe lay on the floor, breath labored as if in pain.

What the fuck? Jagger dropped to his knees beside her, unsure if he should touch her. No movement. That told him she'd passed out from the pain of the change. How had this happened?

Glancing around the room, he spotted a syringe a few feet away. He leaned over and picked up the needle and growled.

"What the hell?" Ayden kneeled down beside him.

"That's what I want to know," Jagger mumbled.

Ayden glanced back at Khloe and hovered his hand above her still cat form. "Well, shit. She's going to be pissed."

Jagger raised an eyebrow at the sheriff, noting he was as freaked as Jagger was. *Fuck.* He scooped her up in his arms and stood.

"Where are you taking her?"

"To the condo. She needs to adjust to her...new form."

Ayden shifted his gaze from Jagger to Khloe. "How long is she going to be like that?"

Jagger sighed, fully understanding why he'd asked. Kalissa would want as many answers as she could get. "I'm not sure. A couple of hours, couple of days. It depends on her ability to control her emotions."

"A couple of days, then."

Jagger nodded. "At least."

"Keep us posted."

"I will." There were a few minutes of silence before Jagger added, "You going to take care of everything here?"

"Yeah." Ayden raised his hand and a small fireball formed in his palm.

Without another word, Jagger teleported to Khloe's condo.

Once safely inside the condo, he laid her in the middle of the bed. His Khloe looked so peaceful and beautiful in her black, and very large, cat form. Her breathing was still labored. He stroked her silky coat, and she calmed.

Thank the gods. She recognized his touch. That meant she hadn't gone insane. He hoped. He would still have to deal with her when she woke. She wasn't going to like this, not one bit.

Willing a blanket from the closet, he draped it over her and snatched up the phone to call her twin.

Kalissa answered after the first ring. "What happened? How is it possible that my sister can shift into a cat?"

Jagger suppressed a growl. "I was hoping you could answer that question for me."

"Me?"

"I need to know your family history. Especially your father's."

"Our father's? He was human."

Clenching the phone a little tighter, he spoke through his teeth. "Are you sure?"

She fell silent for a couple of moments before whispering, "No."

Fuck. Fuck. *Stay calm, Jag. Going all demon isn't going to help Khloe.* "All right. Can you look into it? Find out anything you can about both sides of your family tree."

"Why does any of it matter?"

"Because I need to know if it is an actual wereleopard gene you carry or a demonic one."

A gasp filtered through the phone. "What would happen if the gene is demonic?"

Jagger closed his eyes, and his chest tightened at the fear in her voice. "If Khloe's new shifter abilities are a result of being part demon, we may never be able to bring her back."

CHAPTER TWENTY-THREE

Khloe opened her eyes to a delicious sight and smell. Jagger's bare chest lay against her cheek, and his sandalwood and spice scent invaded her nose. She snuggled farther into him, relishing his warmth. He wrapped his arms around her and kissed her on the top of the head.

She lifted her head and stretched to kiss his lips. Groaning at her aching muscles, the fight at the farmhouse came back to her.

Samoan.

Her words filtered in, bringing back the memory of being injected by something that felt as though she were being turned inside out. The words Samoan had spoken after injecting her flowed inside her mind. It wasn't possible. How could she change into a cat?

Fear flooded her, and she scrambled off the bed. "What did Samoan do to me?"

Rising to his knees on the bed, Jagger peered at her with fear and concern in his expression. This couldn't be good. If the Death Demon was afraid, then the world was about to end. "Listen carefully. It is very important that you remain calm and keep an open mind."

Uh-oh, she wasn't going to like it one bit. "She said my father was part wereleopard." Reality slammed into her as her mind connected with the meaning of the demon's words.

Now you will be one.

She took another couple of steps backward. "This can't happen. It's not possible." The statement came on a growl that sounded too close to that of a cat. She clamped her hand over her mouth.

"If you don't calm down, you'll change again. And it will hurt like hell."

She froze, disbelieving and pissed at the whole situation. Taking several deep breaths, she calmed her irritation, a little. "How is this possible?"

He stood and turned his back on her to stare out the floor-to-ceiling windows. She watched his back muscles tense. He was hiding something.

"Samoan gave you a serum that awakened a gene inside you that allows you to shift."

"A gene? Samoan said my father was a were."

"We're not sure. You could be a wereleopard or something else."

Something else? He believed she was a monster. Fury

burned its way through her veins. How could he say that? What did he mean? Pain gripped her, and she shook. Fuck. It was happening again. "How...do...I stop it?"

He turned to face her, shaking his head. Anger blurred her vision. Every joint in her body ached. Why wasn't he helping her?

His mouth moved, but she couldn't hear him.

An aggression unlike any she had felt before filled her, and the urge to attack was fierce. She fought it, trying to push it back. She called the elements. The French doors flung open, slamming against the walls. Wind blew furiously through the opening. Lightning flashed in the night sky.

But nothing eased the pain or slowed the shift.

No. I'm speeding it up.

Damn it. Jagger did nothing to help.

One last scream ripped from her throat, and she lunged for her prey.

Jagger dodged Khloe as she jumped toward him, her

long, sharp fangs bared as she hissed and growled at him. He tried to calm her, telling her not to resist the change, but she didn't hear him. His heart ached to witness the amount of pain she went through. The first time she'd changed at the farmhouse in Georgia, she hadn't understood what was happening. She still didn't understand it, but she'd known it was coming.

This time, she fought—and fought it hard. That only made the shift into the leopard more painful.

In two strides, he had her pinned to the bed with his body and held her huge cat head in his hands to keep her from biting. He couldn't allow her to take blood this early. She would crave the hunt, and they were in the middle of the city with roughly eight hundred thousand people.

She growled deep in her chest, and her tail slapped against the bed repeatedly.

"You have to calm down." Jagger loosened his grip on her slightly.

Big mistake. Her hind leg kicked him in the groin, loosening his hold more. The sting of sharp teeth puncturing his hand drew a curse from him. He jerked his hand back, and Khloe fled. *Fuck.* She'd drawn blood. Jumping off the bed, he faced her as she panted by the opened French doors. He held a hand out, and she growled and moved back, closer to the balcony.

He stopped and dropped his hand. "Lo. We can work through this. We'll figure it out."

Another growl followed by a hiss was his answer

before she turned, ran, and jumped onto the patio railing. With one last look at him, she jumped.

Jagger screamed her name and rushed to peer over the side of the terrace in time to see her dematerialize. He pushed off the railing when the phone rang. He groaned. *Damn twins and their psychic bonds.*

"She's on the run." No use trying to lie to Kalissa. The witch already knew. Hell, she had probably already tried to link with Khloe and failed.

"I know. She's scared. What the hell is going on?"

Breathe and count to ten. "She's pissed at me, Samoan, the demons...because she doesn't know for sure what is happening to her."

"I know that, too, but what did you do?"

"I tried to calm her. Look, I need to find her. She bit me and could be high on bloodlust."

"I thought only vampires had that."

One...two... "Kalissa, I don't have time to explain things now. I need to find your sister."

A shaky sigh escaped her. Great, an upset pregnant female. "I can't link to her when she's in animal form. I'm assuming she is a cat right now, right?"

"Yes, she is."

Think, damn it. He could find her. She was his mate, after all. But they weren't bonded. He had to try. "I'm going to find her."

He hung up before Kalissa had a chance to reply. Closing his eyes, he concentrated on Khloe, imagined her pink-streaked blond hair and teal eyes. The visual flashed in his mind, only to disappear just as fast.

Pulse thundering in his ears, he couldn't focus. Too much had happened, and there were too many possibilities. *Where the hell would she go?*

Samoan.

The one thing Jagger had learned about Khloe was her impulsive and controlling nature. She was pissed that control had been taken away from her. She would want to hunt down the person responsible.

Without another thought, Jagger willed his body to fade.

Materializing in a dark corner of the Riverwalk on the north bank of the St. Johns River, he inhaled deeply to take in the scents around him. All he could pick up were humans.

He scanned the area as he walked down the sidewalk toward the center of downtown. A few yards away from the busy Riverwalk, he caught a glimpse of a large black blur. Scenting the air confirmed the dark, cat-like figure was Khloe.

He lengthened his strides to catch up with her, but she noticed him and bolted to the other side of the street. With a soft curse, he tried tracking her with little luck. Rounding the next corner, he found himself facing a brick wall. Khloe was nowhere in sight.

Fuck. Where are you, Khloe? How in the hell had she gotten away from him?

A growl followed by a roar echoing off the buildings made his heart seize behind his ribs.

Khloe.

He took off in the direction of the sound. Rounding the corner, he caught a whiff of Khloe's scent mixed with blood. Cold fear and adrenaline raced through his veins. His boots pounded the pavement as he ran at with inhuman speed, following Khloe's growls.

Skidding to a halt at the entrance of the alley, fury burned away his fear. Three demons had Khloe pinned to the ground, fighting to hold her still while Samoan crouched over her with a syringe.

The demoness snapped her head up in his direction, her cobalt-blue eyes darkening as she smiled at him and plunged the needle into Khloe's neck. With an evil laugh, she whispered, "It's too late, Death."

They vanished, taking Khloe with them.

Khloe's eyes fluttered opened, and she squeezed them shut when the blinding light made her head feel like it would split open. She stretched out her tight, sore muscles and groaned at the feel of concrete against bare skin. Awareness filtered into her fuzzy memory of how she'd been captured.

She'd been in cat form, pissed, unsure how to change back. As she'd padded through the downtown streets, trying to clear her head and figure out what the hell was going on, she came across a group of demons. They instantly knew who and what she was and attacked.

Stupid, impulsive witch. She shouldn't have lashed out at Jagger. She knew in her heart he had only been trying to help, but her fear of the unknown and anger at her parents for not sharing an important piece of her genetic makeup overrode her ability to reason.

Opening her eyes slowly, she took in her surroundings. The first thing she noticed was the bars.

Just freaking great. She was naked, cold, and locked behind bars like the animal stirring inside her.

Scanning beyond the circus hotel, she saw computers and high-tech lab equipment. Light reflected off something on the table to her right. Focusing on the object, she shifted closer to the bars. Dread washed through her. It was a crystal very similar to the one that hung around Jagger's neck and a smaller version of the one in Teddy-Bear's possession.

Fuck. How in the hell did the demons get a piece of the Sinew? Even more important, how many fragments were out there?

Footsteps had her shrink back and pretend to sleep.

"Has she been able to transfer the power to the stone?"

A deep, husky voice boomed through the quiet lab and made Khloe's skin crawl. Demetrius. *Bastard.*

"No. She isn't strong enough." The *Lackey* picked up the stone and slipped it into his pocket. "Of course, she could be faking."

Demetrius shook his head, disappointment coloring his expression. "No, I considered that. She is strong enough. She just doesn't know it."

When the demon general moved toward the cell, she closed her eyes and forced her breathing to slow. That was hard to do with their words swirling inside her mind. They had a witch working for them. It was the only possibility. But what did they mean about transferring power?

CHAPTER TWENTY-FOUR

Kalissa sat at a large, rectangular table in Noah and Vanessa's library, staring absently at the computer screen and going through the coven's archives. "I can't believe he never told us." The man she'd loved and admired all her life had lied to her or, at the very least, had withheld a very important chunk of her heritage from her and her twin. Their father was half leopard-shifter, and she and Khloe carried the gene. The knowledge infuriated her and hurt like hell.

Vanessa's warm hand covered hers. "His family cut all ties to him when he married your mother."

Shock drew her focus to her mother's best friend, but Kalissa should have known that the priestess would know. "That's not a very good excuse to keep it from us."

"I agree, and I tried to talk to your mother about it. Khloe has shown signs of aggression and dominance her whole life. When you both went through puberty without going through the change, I stopped worrying so much. I still expressed my feelings about keeping this from you, but she thought she was protecting you." Vanessa paused and released a sigh before continuing. "We were all wrong. We should have known the demons would use it against you."

Letting everything settle in, she refocused on the computer. Her hand drifted to her still flat stomach, and she lifted her gaze to Vanessa. "What about my child?"

Longing and a hint of sadness passed over Vanessa's features but vanished seconds later. "There is always a chance your children will be able to shift, but now that the demons injected the gene enhancer into Lo, her children will have a greater chance than yours."

A laugh bubbled up, and Kalissa didn't hold it in. "Can you see Lo having children?"

Vanessa smiled. "She's not the mothering type, is she?"

"Not really. She loves children, but doesn't have the slightest interest in having any of her own." The image of her twin chasing after a couple of cubs amused her more than it should.

The slam of the front door followed by heavy footsteps brought their attention to the living room entrance. Ayden rushed in, his eyes fixing on hers. "They took Lo."

Kalissa stood and moved toward him. He stopped her by wrapping his arms around her waist, holding her in place. "You're not going," he said firmly into her hair. Tears spilled over her lids.

"Who's going?"

"Jagger, Lex, and Zach are already downtown." He pulled her away from him enough to lock gazes. "I can't risk anything happening to you or the baby."

She pressed a finger to his lips. "I know." She wrapped her arms around his waist and pressed her cheek to his chest. "I'll have to trust that Death Demon to protect his mate."

Khloe thought the demons would never leave. Her self-control had truly been tested moments ago when Demetrius had poked her through the bars with something unknown, but she was sure she didn't want to know what it was. She'd really wanted to lash out and set his demon-ass on fire along with the whole building. But, she couldn't do that until she found out if that stone was indeed a piece of the Sinew and what the demons had planned for it.

First, she had to get the hell out of this damn cell.

Pushing to a stand, she instinctively tried to teleport. She wasn't too surprised to find a spell in place to keep unwanted beings out or, in her case, to keep magical prisoners in. However, the spell was placed around the building and not the cage. A smirk lifted one corner of her mouth as she flashed to stand on the other side of the bars.

Demons just weren't very smart at times.

She conjured clothes on her body and went to the computer, and giddiness rose in her chest. Fingers flying over the keys, she worked to break the code and gain access to the files.

Ten minutes later, she was in, and disappointment weighed on her. Every file was encrypted. *Shit*. It'd take her all night to break each one. Opening her on-line email account, she compressed the files and sent them to Zach. Hopefully, he would recognize them for what they were.

A noise outside the door pushed her into action. She was not going to be tranquilized again and shoved back into the oversized animal cage. A shiver went through her as the fear of being caught changed to determination. The cat within agreed that they would fight to keep from being contained again.

She'd crept a few feet to the door on the other side

of the lab when she doubled over from muscle spasms. *No, no, no. Not now. We need to get out of here.* She started to shake, and panic set in. That was how they'd caught her in the first place. *Stupid cat.*

Think. She had to calm herself. When she'd lost consciousness under the drug they'd given her, she'd shifted. Earlier, her anger toward Jagger and Samoan had caused her to shift. It made sense that the change was controlled by her emotions.

Okay, kitty. We have to work together. I need my legs to kick that she-demon-elf-bitch's ass. So work with me.

The small spasms slowed until her muscles relaxed enough to walk. She guessed that was some kind of progress. Before she could reach the rear exit, the other door crashed open. The leopard growled in her mind, and Khloe glared at Samoan standing in the doorway, alone.

"I see the kitty is out of her cage," Samoan purred and inched closer, manifesting a dagger in her right hand.

Nice.

"May the Goddess give me strength." Khloe felt a rush of power roll through her, but it wasn't from Hecate answering her prayer. This was natural, primal, and raw. The same power she possessed in leopard form. *Nice. Good kitty.*

"Thanks for the gift, Samoan."

Their mother had always told the twins to accept their gifts as a link to their inner strengths, and feel the power in every pore of their being. The magic was their lifeline, their souls. She had always felt something else deeper within her but had never known what it was, until now.

The demoness snarled. "It wasn't a fucking gift, bitch. Why can't you witches do anything you're supposed to do?"

"Now that wouldn't be any fun. You should know that I never play by the rules."

"Yes, you're a freak of nature."

"That I will have to agree with you on." Khloe raised her hands. The few large, rectangular windows several inches from the ceiling opened, and the wind blew around the room, scattering papers.

Thrusting one hand out, Khloe levitated a chair and flung it at Samoan. The demoness dodged it and returned the favor by hurling a small table at her. Khloe jumped out of the way, which gave the demon-bitch time to charge her.

Samoan hit her in the side like a linebacker sacking a quarterback. Pain sliced through Khloe's ribs as they hit the floor in a tangle of arms and legs then rolled until Khloe pinned the she-demon. Samoan back-handed her, sending Khloe to the floor. The female demon rolled to her side and pushed to a stand. Khloe kicked out, hitting Samoan in the knee. Samoan cried out as she fell and her back slammed into the ground. Jumping up, Khloe picked up the dagger Samoan had dropped. Snatching her up by her ponytail, Khloe pressed the knife to Samoan's throat.

A scream ripped from Khloe, and she crumbled to ground, every muscle convulsing painfully. Footfalls sounded around her, and then voices erupted into a clatter of noise. She lost focus. Her skin tightened, but this time, she didn't fight the change. No, she accepted it, wanted it, and vowed to her leopard never to keep her penned up again.

Jagger led Lex and Zach through the basement of the warehouse, following his mate's scent. It carried a heavier scent of rose than usual. She was pissed but alive. He reached the end of the corridor at the same time the sound of a scream cut into his heart.

He rounded the corner to see Khloe fall to her knees, a demon standing behind her with his hands outstretched. Samoan staggered to her feet, but Jagger's focus was on his mate struggling for control as she shook wildly while her body shifted into her leopard.

He took a step but stopped when the male demon snapped his gaze toward him and raised his arms, ready to fire. If it were only him, he wouldn't give a shit. He'd take out the whole damn place. With one flick of the wrist, the building could be engulfed in flames. He could handle the Fire, unlike his brother, mate, and Zach.

Seconds later, a black leopard let out a roar and twisted to lunge at the demon behind her.

"Damn. That is going to take some getting used to," Zach said beside him, the tone of his voice a mixture of proud brother and pissed-off witch.

Jagger couldn't have agreed more.

"The cavalry has arrived," Lex's flat tone warned from behind them.

Jagger turned to peer over his shoulder. Five large *Amiddians* stormed into the room. As a unit, Jagger, Zach, and Lex turned to face the group. The wall of hairless creatures wore blank expressions. Jagger wondered if these were the power-enhanced scouts Ryn had mentioned. They were nothing but puppets, and Khan pulled the strings.

Not feeling even a smidgen of pity, Jagger thrust an energy bolt at them. It hit the biggest demon and propelled him backward into a glass cabinet. Shattering glass bounced across the floor and tables nearby, and the demon dropped to the floor. Calling the element of Fire, Jag finished the bastard off by blasting him with a fireball.

Lex and Zach split off from him, each taking on a demon in hand-to-hand combat.

A blur of black fur flew by him and pounced on one of the other males. Trusting his mate to hold her own, he turned to face the fifth demon, who stood staring, unblinking. Jagger raised more energy to get ready to blast him. The demon must have sensed it because he crouched, ready to charge.

Jagger braced for impact, wanting to get his hands on the demon. Hitting him full force, the demon blasted him with more power than an average *Amiddian* should have possessed. Jagger fell to his knees, howling from the pain as the electrical current surged through his nervous system. A sharp stab in his chest drew his attention downward. A wicked smile formed on his lips. "You'll have to do better than that, asshole."

Thrusting his hand out, Jagger snatched the demon by the throat, and with a flick of the wrist, snapped the bastard's neck. He tossed the lifeless body to the ground just as more demons entered the room. Samoan laughed and ordered, "Get her," before tele-porting out.

The demons pinned Khloe with glares and raised their arms. Dark magic stirred within the room. The air, charged with Fire magic, told Jagger they were calling demon fire—a white-hot, magical blast that in small doses would wound even a god, but a large enough dose could kill one. Jagger screamed, but Khloe was too engaged with the demon she fought. Distracted and in cat form, unaware.

There was only one thing to do. To save her.

Jagger flashed to stand in front her. The demon fire hit his chest, throwing him across the room. Unlike normal fire, the dark blast burned from the inside. He screamed, trying to will the fire out of him. It was no use. Pain overrode thoughts and the ability to effectively use his powers. Darkness closed in around him and dragged him under.

Jagger's pained screams sliced Khloe's heart. She yowled and ran to his too-still form on the floor. Blood streamed out of his ears. Her heart shattered into pieces as she shifted back to her human body. She rolled him onto his back and caressed his face with her fingers. He was hot. Too hot.

With a scream of her own, she whirled around and faced the wall of demons staring at her like a bunch of idiots. "Fucking die, bastards!" She threw her hands out, calling to Fire and wind, and directing the flames at them. Then she opened the link to her brother-in-law's gift of adaptability. Searching the demon's powers, she found the link that allowed them to call the demon fire and used it, burning the fuckers from the inside while the natural flames burned them from the outside.

Movement behind her made her turn and hiss at whoever approached.

Lex stared, unfazed by her primal attempt to protect her mate. His chest rose and fell, and his crimson eyes glistened in the light. It was the most emotion the demon had shown since she'd met him, but Khloe smelled the pain and fear drifting from him.

Footsteps behind her made her pivot around, ready to attack, but it was Zach. All the demons were dead. Samoan, on the other hand, had flashed out moments before Jagger was hit. That bitch was hers, and Khloe would get her revenge. Some day.

Bringing her attention back to Lex, she pleaded with tears rolling down her cheeks, "Fix him. You have the power to give him life."

Moisture in his eyes increased, and he shook his head. "Jagger has that gift, not me. There is no cure for demon fire." He bent down and lifted his brother in his arms.

No. Jagger has to pull out of it. "Call Hecate. There has to be something we can do. What about the Fates?"

Lex just gave a nod. Khloe wanted to scream at him,

hit him. But deep down, she knew he was right. Demon fire was lethal even to the gods.

Cotton touched her bare skin. Startled, she peered at Zach. He had taken his button-up shirt off and draped it over her shoulders. Sliding her arms into the sleeves, she sniffed with a soft "thank you" and allowed him to lead her out the door.

"Goddess, please bring him back to me."

CHAPTER TWENTY-FIVE

"*L*o, hon. You need to rest."

Khloe shook her head and continued to wipe Jagger's brow with a cool cloth, speaking to him in hushed tones. His fever had finally broken two days before, but she wanted him to know she was there and wouldn't leave. Hecate was able to stop the demon fire the night they'd brought him home, but he hadn't shown any signs of waking. "I'll sleep when I know he'll be all right."

Lydia laid her hand on Jagger's chest and sighed. The healer didn't need to say it. Khloe knew. No change.

"Why hasn't he woken up? It's been five days."

"There was a lot of internal damage," Lydia replied, but Khloe could tell the healer didn't have any answers.

Khloe lay down beside him and rested her head on his chest. His heart thumped in a steady pace but didn't soothe her like it should. She released a shaky breath and snuggled into him. "Please, come back to me."

Jagger floated. At least, it seemed like he was on a bed of air, light, and in no hurry to get anywhere. Where was he? Darkness surrounded him.

Please come back to me. The words whispered to his subconscious. Khloe?

Then the events replayed in his mind. Demons flooding the room with one target in their sights. Then Jagger jumping in the line of fire, taking the full force of the demon fire aimed right at his mate.

Khan had gone from capturing Khloe to kill order? Or was it Samoan's order?

How was he still alive? Well, not really alive. But not dead either.

A soft white light shone above him. A familiar face appeared. Her hair was black as night and her eyes were green like emeralds. Two other females hung behind her, not coming too close, but Jagger sensed they were there.

The Fates.

The female closest to him spoke softly. "Hello, my son."

"Have you come to take me like you took my family?" he couldn't keep the harshness out of his words. "Why have you cursed me? Am I not allowed to love?"

He didn't want her there. His soul would soon go to the Elysian Fields. That thought broke his heart. Khloe. He'd never see her, touch her, smell her again.

"My son, I do not control all things. Just the path and keeping the balance."

He let out a growl. "Leave."

A soft sob escaped her, and she stepped closer. "I come to give you a gift."

He laughed bitterly. "At what cost?"

"Your life for your immortality."

Narrowing his eyes, he focused on her face as he sat up. "What are you saying?"

"You can go back to your mate, but you will be mortal. You and Khloe can bond, and you'll take her lifespan. However, when she dies, so will you." The goddess of Fate blinked then lifted the corners of her mouth. "You sacrificed your life for hers and have suffered so much loss. I haven't been there, couldn't interfere. But I can give you this gift. If you accept."

He'd give anything to be with Khloe. Giving up his powers was a big sacrifice, but he'd do it. He'd share her lifespan, and they'd go into the afterlife together... "Wait. I thought the Divinities were immortal?"

"No. They have extended lifespans. Many will live for thousands of years, but they can be killed. With the war between witches and demons, there is no guarantee how long Khloe's life will be." She frowned and lowered her green gaze. "I'm sorry, I wish there was more I could do."

Jagger nodded, hope restoring in his heart. "I will need my Death Demon strengths and powers to help the Divinities fight in this war. I'll give up my immortality and god powers I've gained from you and Hecate."

"Done." She leaned in and kissed his forehead.

As soon as she stepped away from him, she was gone, and the darkness faded into the soft glow of Khloe's bathroom light spilling into the bedroom. The scents of chocolate and roses filled the room. His chest tightened, and tears filled his eyes.

Khloe's soft snores were like music to his ears. He gathered her in his arms and held her close, not wanting to let her go. Ever.

Warmth enveloped her and soft lips pressed against her forehead. Khloe sighed and snuggled into Jagger more. She never wanted to wake from this dream.

"Welcome back to the living, brother."

Lex's voice made her open her eyes on a start. She lifted her head and met the most captivating chocolate-brown gaze. Jagger's sensual lips lifted in a smile, and she peppered him with kisses. Tears spilled over her eyes and streamed down her cheeks. "I almost lost you." Pulling back to give him a stern stare, she demanded, "Don't ever scare me like that again."

He chuckled. "I don't plan on it." Cupping her face, he drew her to him for a deep kiss.

Kalissa cleared her throat from the door. Khloe glanced back at her twin and smiled. She carried a tray of food and water.

"Lex verified that there was a piece of the Sinew lost and that it is possible it was broken off when the demons last had possession of it." Kalissa sat the tray on the nightstand and moved to sit in the chair next to the window.

Jagger looked puzzled, so Khloe told him about the stone she'd seen in the lab, and what the demons had said about transferring power to it.

"I've had my suspicions. The *Amiddians* are much stronger than they should be. Whatever witch they have in their possession can't possibly be able to transfer magic into it unless they are a god or goddess."

Jagger shook his head. "There's no way. They'd need at least a couple of first-generation Divinities."

First-generation? Khloe's mind turned over all kinds of possibilities. "Mel? Are you or Noah first-generation?"

"I never gave it much thought. Noah has always kept up with that information."

Zach cleared his throat. "Noah is."

Khloe studied him. "Are you sure?"

Avoiding her gaze, he nodded. She had always suspected Zach hid secrets. In fact, she had observed several oddities about her best friend over the years. But it had only been recently that he'd acted a little more aggressive on their demon hunts. Not to mention that the level of power he carried had increased.

Her new leopard senses allowed her to pick up on emotions by scent, and her connection to Jagger allowed her to gauge others' power levels better. She was ten times more powerful, both magically and physically. It was all a little frightening.

Lydia rocked her son and patted his back as she spoke. "We have to get the stone from them, whether it's an active section of the Sinew or not. They can't be allowed to test it or whatever they have planned for it."

"Lydia is right," Kalissa said.

Khloe nodded. "So we go get it."

Everyone turned to her as if waiting for her to jump up and run out the door. Not happening. She didn't need to. "I'm blaming the cat for the need to plan and stalk before attacking." She smiled, and the cat purred in her head.

Kalissa laughed. "We have to record this. It's a historic moment."

"Ha, ha." Khloe threw the spare pillow at her. Looking back at her mate, she confessed, "Kris has been working with me on controlling the shift and my new senses and strength. I still have a lot to learn, but the old jump-in-ask-questions-later Khloe is fading." Plus, she had a godson to help protect, and a nephew on the way. It was time to take on responsibilities. "Plus, it's much more effective to kick demon ass when you have the upper hand."

Jagger tugged Khloe into his arms to capture her lips. She pressed into him, and a purr rumbled from her chest onto his. Chuckling, he broke the kiss and held her face in his hands. Her teal-colored eyes shone with a hint of tears, and his heart skipped a beat. Dread enveloped him. "What's wrong?"

Kalissa made a soft noise. One-by-one, everyone

said their goodnights and left the room. "Call when you two come up for air." She walked to the door and turned back to them. "Welcome to the family, Jagger."

The door closed with a soft click as he shifted his gaze back to Khloe, now smiling above him. "Is that what the watery eyes were for a few moments ago?"

Biting her bottom lip, she nodded and lowered her head to his. He rose up just enough to gently bite her chin. Her cry of shock made him chuckle. He rolled her to her back.

Her eyes held laughter and desire. "I love you, Jag."

Rising up, he stared down at her. Love filled his heart and spread like a warm current in his veins. "I love you, too. And have since the first day I saw you." Her bottom lip trembled, and he kissed it then slid his lips down her throat.

"Jagger?"

"Yes?"

"When were you going to tell me we're half-mated?"

His body chilled. *Shit.* He'd forgotten about taking her blood. Meeting her gaze, relief that she wasn't angry filled him, and he relaxed. No, she wasn't mad, but she was annoyed. He had learned that it was better to have an annoyed Khloe than a pissed-off one. "I... All I thought about when I took your blood was that you would live. I wasn't prepared to lose you."

Her brows drew together. "And were you prepared to never mate another again?"

Blowing out a breath, he confessed, "There would

never be anyone else for me as long as you live, with or without your blood inside me."

She fell silent for several moments, and he feared what she would say. When her teal stare turned a darker green, and a smile lifted the corners of her lips, hope bloomed inside him. "You died. I felt you slip away."

Closing his eyes briefly he drew her into a tight hug, kidding the top of her head. "I'm not immortal anymore. I had to give up my powers of Fate to return to you."

"Your mother...?"

"Yes. She *gifted* me a life with you."

Khloe lifted her head and frowned while crinkling her nose. "A gift with conditions. How thoughtful."

Jagger framed her face in his hands. "I'll take it any way I can get it."

Khloe sighed. "I guess. Hey, what happens when we mate? I mean, is your lifespan shorter now?"

"I will take your lifespan."

A wide smile formed on her lips and she crawled up to nip at his bottom lip. "In that case, what are we waiting for? Let's complete the mating. I want to be yours for the rest of our existence."

A growl of desire hung in the back of his throat. "And I want to be yours, as well."

He'd raised his wrist to bite down when she stopped him. "What are you doing?"

"To complete the bond, you need to drink my blood."

She smiled wide enough for him to see her small, sharp, leopard fangs. Damn, she was sexy as hell. He pressed his hard cock against her jeans. She groaned and removed her clothes by magic and sank her fangs into his neck.

An uncontrollable amount of desire flooded his senses. He entered her with a quick thrust and stilled. He didn't want to come yet. It was hard not to with her warm, wet pussy clutching his dick and her fangs inside him. Her gentle pulls as she drank were more arousing than he'd ever dreamt.

She withdrew from him and licked the puncture marks. He shivered. "What?"

"Your tongue. It's rough, like a cat's."

She laughed. "Apparently, that is the only thing that doesn't shift back. Does it bother you?"

"No. It's cute." She started to push against him, but he thrust deeper inside her, making her gasp in pleasure. "It's a part of who you are now. I love everything about you."

He kissed her, not giving her time to respond. Slipping his tongue between her lips, he moved his cock in and out of her until they cried out in release.

Rolling to his back, he positioned Khloe to drape over his chest and rubbed her back in circular motions. "So, how soon are we going after the crystal the demons have?"

Shrugging, she wiggled into him a little more. A wicked gleam sparked in her teal gaze. "Oh, I don't know. You did die. I think it would be wise for you to stay in bed for at least another week. Maybe a month."

He raised an eyebrow. "Just how do you plan on keeping me here?"

She lifted her head and crawled up his body to straddle him. "I can think of a few ways."

"What if I'm not the easiest patient?"

Leaning down, she nipped his lip. "I'll be forced to tie you down."

He wrapped his fingers around the back of her neck and drew her to him. "I love you."

"Love you, too. Always."

EPILOGUE

*S*amoan stormed into the lab with a target in sight. The witch sat in the love seat, reading, all comfortable as though she weren't in a building full of demons. That pissed Samoan off, which was why the bitch did it.

And she couldn't kill the *Porter*. Damn it.

"How did your visit with your son go?"

"Not long enough." Her complaint was the same as always, void of emotion.

"You still haven't given me any information. You're lucky you got to see the brat in the first place." The witch glared, and Samoan laughed. "Nothing is free, witch."

"I told you, I don't know anything."

"I think you're lying."

"The Divinities have been busy with your stunt involving Khloe and the birth of Lydia's son."

Samoan froze. "Lydia's son? Is he a Dark Divine?"

The female paled, giving Samoan the answer she wanted. Demetrius had said Lydia had been born of two first-generation Divinities and that the child's father was a demon.

"That's not what I said. You're putting words in my mouth."

"And you are a terrible liar."

Samoan turned to leave, only to have the witch attack her. They hit the floor, and Samoan flipped her onto her back to hold the Divinity by her throat. "Any more of that and you will never see your son again."

The sound of footsteps rang out as demons rushed into the room. Samoan pulled the witch to a stand by her hair and shoved her toward a demon. "Lock her up."

When they left, Samoan pulled out her cell and punched in her father's number. He answered on the second ring. "The child has arrived."

Continue The Divinities series with book 3, Dark Divine
Coming November 2016

Get updates on releases via Lia's newsletter
https://www.subscribepage.com/authorliadavis

ABOUT LIA DAVIS

USA Today bestselling author Lia Davis spends most of her time writing racy romance and witty women's fiction, the majority of which takes place in fantasy worlds full of magic and mayhem. She prides herself on her ability to craft strong and sassy heroines, emotionally intelligent alpha heroes, and rich, expansive universes that readers want to visit again and again.

She is the mastermind behind the bestselling Ashwood Falls Series and the co-author of the beloved Witching After Forty Series.

She currently resides in Florida where she's working on her very own happily-ever-after with her supportive husband and spends her free time doting on a pack of feisty felines and her loving family.

Find all of Lia's online hangouts here:
https://solo.to/authorliadavis
Check out the official Davis Raynes Merch Etsy Store:
https://www.etsy.com/shop/davisraynesmerch

ALSO BY LIA DAVIS

Paranormal Women's Fiction

Witching After Forty (Co-written with L.A. Boruff)

Fanged After Forty (Co-written with L.A. Boruff)

Shifting Through Midlife (Co-written with L.A. Boruff and Lacey Carter)

Packless in Seattle

Paranormal Romance Series

Shifters of Ashwood Falls

Bears of Blackrock

Dragons of Ares

Gods and Dragons

Dark Scales Division (Co-written with Kerry Adrienne)

Shifting Magick Trilogy

The Divinities

Witches of Rose Lake

Coven's End (Co-written with L.A. Boruff)

Academy's Rise (Co-written with L.A. Boruff)

Wolf Ranch

Singles Titles

First Contact (MM co-written with Kerry Adrienne)

Ghost in the Bottle (co-written with Kerry Adrienne)

Dragon's Web

Royal Enchantment

Marked by Darkness

His Big Bad Wolf (MM)

Their Royal Ash

Tempting the Wolf

Hexed with Sass (part of the Milly Taiden Sassy Ever After World)

Claiming Her Dragons (Part of the Milly Taiden Paranormal Dating Agency)

Rogue Alliance (Part of the Wolves of Chaos Valley Shared World)

Rune of Passing (Part of the Immortal Keepers Shared World)

Contemporaries

Pleasures of the Heart Series

Single Titles

His Guarded Heart (MM)